The California Kid Fights Back

Don't Miss the First Adventure
of Flattop Kincaid in
THE KID WHO GOT ZAPPED THROUGH TIME
by Deborah Scott
from Avon Camelot

DEBORAH SCOTT graduated from college with a double major in English and Theater Arts that led to a double career path. She has worked as a comedienne and as a writer for television, radio and film. At the same time, she was a substitute teacher for middle school and junior high. *The Kid Who Got Zapped Through Time* was her first novel for middle-grade readers. Ms. Scott lives in the Tehachapi Mountains in California with her husband, David Hall.

The California Kid Fights Back

DEBORAH SCOTT

AN AVON CAMELOT BOOK

For the kids of the Torrance and Tehachapi School Districts.

AVON BOOKS, INC.
1350 Avenue of the Americas
New York, New York 10019

Copyright © 1998 by Deborah Scott
Published by arrangement with the author
Visit our website at http://www.AvonBooks.com
Library of Congress Catalog Card Number: 98-92785
ISBN: 0-380-72851-6

First Avon Camelot Printing: September 1998

CAMELOT TRADEMARK REG. U.S. PAT. OFF. AND IN OTHER COUNTRIES, MARCA REGISTRADA, HECHO EN U.S.A.

Printed in the U.S.A.

OPM   10 9 8 7 6 5 4 3 2 1

The Robber King grabbed the collar of Flattop Kincaid's red satin jacket and yanked him closer. "So, lad, you think you can get rid of me that easily, eh?" Flattop winced, partly because he was afraid and partly because the Robber King's breath smelled like dirty socks.

"You—you're dead!" Flattop protested.

The Robber King's mouth turned upward in an evil grin. "So are you." He wrapped his grimy, fat fingers around Flattop's throat and began to squeeze.

Flattop tried to yell for help, but the words wouldn't come. He twisted his head from side to side and struggled to tear the Robber King's hands from his throat.

As the villain's grip grew tighter, Flattop thrashed backward and shouted, "Noooo!"

His eyes flew open, and he looked around hoping to find a way to escape. But instead of the Robber King's camp, he discovered he was in English class. With everyone staring at him. Ms. McVey scowled. "Is something wrong, Mr. Kincaid?"

"No . . ." Flattop paused. He couldn't say he'd fallen asleep because he was bored. And he couldn't tell her the truth—that he'd just gotten back from the Middle Ages, and time travel made him tired.

He looked down at his open grammar book and felt his cheeks get hot as the kids began to giggle and whisper. Even his best friend Jason was laughing. He waited for Ms. McVey to yell at him. But she continued her lecture on adding an *e-d* to make a verb past tense.

Flattop breathed a sigh of relief and closed his eyes. In an instant, his brain filled with images—faces that appeared and disappeared like ghosts. He saw the Wizard, dressed in a jogging suit, selling him a computer game at the swap meet. *You want an adventure, my boy,* the old man had said.

Flattop had gotten an adventure all right. He'd been sucked through his computer to England in the year 1150 A.D., to eat endless bowls of porridge with a family of serfs. John, Ruth, and their three kids thought Flattop's red satin jacket meant he was rich and powerful. If they'd known he was just a scared kid who wanted to go home they probably would've laughed at him. Instead, they thought he was an orphan whose parents had been killed by the Robber King—

Flattop shuddered at the thought of the man's snarling, bearded face, then opened his eyes to escape the images he'd conjured in his own head.

Ms. McVey asked the class, "What's the past tense of 'save?' "

Hoping to get on her good side again, Flattop raised his hand. "Saved," he answered.

"Very good, Mr. Kincaid," she said. "Can you use it in a sentence?"

Tthhhunk! The sound of an arrow as it pierces a man's heart echoed in his brain. The Robber King's dead body falling on him as he struggled to get away. Panic raced through Flattop's body just as it had the day the Robber King had taken him hostage. He could

2

feel beads of sweat form on his forehead and he found it hard to catch his breath.

"Mr. Kincaid?" Ms. McVey prompted.

Flattop clenched his fists so hard, he could feel his arms shake. "The—The squire . . . saved . . . me from the Robber King." In the dead quiet of the classroom he could hear himself panting.

The lunch bell rang.

Ms. McVey dismissed the class and the uneasy silence was replaced by the sounds of chairs scooting away from desks, lunch sacks being yanked out of backpacks, and kids stampeding out the door.

Flattop wiped his sweaty palms on his jeans, then closed his book and put it away. There was no need to run out of the classroom like everyone else. He'd forgotten his lunch. He could call his mom and ask her to bring it, but he wasn't even hungry now. He was almost out the classroom door when he heard Ms. McVey ask him, "Is everything okay, Marvin?"

Flattop winced at his real name. Not only did he like his nickname better, but Ms. McVey called every kid "Miss" or "Mister." When she used a kid's first name it meant they were either in trouble or looked sick.

He hoped he looked sick.

"Marvin?" she asked again. "Are you all right?"

A tiny ray of hope glowed somewhere deep in his chest. He looked sick. He turned to her with half-closed eyes and sighed. "I don't feel very good."

"Maybe you ought to go to the office and call your mom."

"Yeah." Flattop nodded. "Maybe I'll do that." Instead he headed toward the cafeteria.

Ever since last night, when he'd returned from the Middle Ages, things hadn't gone right. His mom lectured him for flushing the toilet over and over, watching the water whoosh away. Obviously she had no idea what life was like in a world of chamber pots and crouching behind bushes.

Now Ms. McVey thought he was sick, and all the kids had laughed at him for acting weird. He may have come back to his own century safe and sound, but inside he wasn't the same.

Flattop paused at the door of the cafeteria. The benches were in rows, like the ones in the Great Hall at Hemstead castle. He watched kids trading the food in their lunches for food some other mom packed. One girl jumped up and tossed the rest of her chips in the trash.

Flattop thought about John and Ruth's seven-year-old daughter Margaret, back in the Middle Ages. Serfs like Margaret's family starved unless they could get jobs working in the castle. Here, people threw away chips because they were barbecue flavored instead of sour cream and onion.

"Hey, Flattop!" his friend Jason called to him from their usual lunch table. "Over here!" Flattop looked at the rest of his friends. Eric was bobbing up and down while he drank from his water bottle, and Sean and Nathan were having a carrot-stick sword fight.

When Flattop had been in the Middle Ages he'd sometimes felt like an outsider. But now he felt worse. His dad had told him once about jet lag. He said a person's body clock got messed up when they traveled across time zones and it made them feel funny. Maybe he had a kind of jet lag. Time lag. Something.

"What're you standing there for?" Jason yelled. "Come on!"

Flattop shook his head and yelled back. "Ms. McVey

says I'm sick and I should go home." That wasn't how the conversation *really* went, but it sounded better to have a teacher's approval if you wanted to go home.

"Okay. Whatever," Jason said, as Eric slammed his fist into Jason's creme-filled cupcake.

The *sploosh* of white cupcake guts all over Jason's lunch sack was pretty funny, even though they were wasting food. Flattop was still smiling when he walked past the office and down a wing of classrooms to the empty playground. Sitting with the cold wall of the building at his back and the wet grass underneath him, Flattop put his hands in his jacket to keep them warm. His fingers wrapped around the apple he'd stuck in his pocket at Hemstead Castle just before the Wizard blasted him back to his century. It was the only proof he'd been there at all.

He pulled it out of his pocket and rubbed his thumb across the red skin. Warm memories flooded his heart. He remembered the night he and Alice sat in the castle kitchen talking about loyalty, chivalry and the dubbing of her husband's brother, William of Wickshire. He wondered if she'd had her baby yet, and if it had her green eyes.

Alice's eyes were the color of Flattop's best cat's-eye marble. He'd never seen eyes that color before. And they sparkled when she laughed. The first time she met him, she stuck her hand out and Flattop didn't know whether he was supposed to kiss it or shake it. So he kissed it. She laughed so much her eyes looked like they had glitter in them.

Even though Alice was twenty-four years old, she didn't talk to him like he was a little kid. He suspected she was nice to everyone, whether they were kids or grown-ups or serfs or nobles.

William was a little snobby when it came to serfs—but he was still a good friend. *The squire saved me from the Robber King.* Yep. That was William.

If it hadn't been for William's quick action, Flattop would've been killed in his own game. But they both survived and William was dubbed a knight. Flattop sighed. It was only moments after the dubbing when he caught the Wizard, touched the dark glass to the old man's hand, and ended the game. Next thing he knew, he was home.

Flattop looked up to see kids pushing and shoving each other on their way to the playground. Some kids from Ms. McVey's class were huddled on the basketball court, whispering and pointing at him. He frowned and lightly twisted the apple stem. The year 1150 A.D. had been a pretty nice place to visit. Nicer than Thomas Jefferson Middle School, where kids laughed at him because he happened to close his eyes for a few seconds.

The grass is always greener on the other side of the fence, his mom always said. While he was back in 1150 A.D., all he thought about was going home to telephones, microwave ovens, and corn dogs. And he'd spent a lot of time worrying about whether his mom and dad had discovered he was gone. And he practically prayed he'd get to see his older sister Marcia again. Hard to believe that now.

Flattop studied a brown speck on the apple. Of course, life as a serf wasn't all that great, eating garbage the nobles threw away. And having the Robber King hold him at knifepoint just to get his red satin jacket wasn't any fun, either. Even at Hemstead Castle where the rich nobles lived, the floors were crawling with fleas and lice.

Still . . . it was a castle.

Flattop rested his head against the school building and closed his eyes. A mental picture of the uneven stone walls and the stinky, brown-foam moat popped into his head. The castle may not have been like the movies, but it was the closest thing to the knights-in-shining-armor stories he'd always heard about. He imagined himself dressed in chain mail and a tunic, sword fighting, riding in a tournament, jousting—

Flattop sat up straight and opened his eyes. "Wait a minute," he declared. "I got cheated!"

After days of sweating in the fields, after nights of sleeping on a table with a serf's whole family, after an agonizing afternoon in the clutches of the Robber King, Flattop had caught the Wizard, won the game—and gone home!

Oh sure, he'd seen William become a knight, but he'd missed the big party. He'd missed congratulating William. Most of all he'd missed having a real-live knight for a friend. Flattop clunked his head against the concrete wall. *Stupid!* He should've hung around William for awhile. Maybe become a knight himself. They could've been knight buddies, riding through the countryside, saving people, and doing good deeds. *Sir Flattop.*

Not bad.

A rumble echoed in his empty stomach. He was hungry after all. He turned his Middle Ages apple over in his hands. It was smaller than the ones his mom got at the store—and the red color was dull. But it would keep his stomach from growling. He rubbed it back and forth on his jacket and inspected the shine.

Uncooked apples are poison, Alice had warned. "Yeah, right," he mumbled to himself, smiling. He opened his mouth to take a bite, but stopped before his teeth broke the skin. Maybe apples in the Middle Ages *were* poisonous. Snow White almost died from a poison apple. Maybe that story came from the Middle Ages. And even if it wasn't poisonous back then, it was hundreds of years old now. Stuff in his own refrigerator got rotten after a couple weeks.

He decided he wasn't that hungry after all and tucked the apple back into his jacket pocket.

"There you are!" A voice startled him out of his thoughts. "I've been looking all over for you."

Flattop looked up to find Alison Wedertz standing over him with one hand on her hip and a disgusted look on her face. "What do you want?" Flattop grumbled.

"You were supposed to meet me in front of Mrs. Penn's class so we could get a head start on our report."

Flattop furrowed his brow. "Report?"

Alison sighed and rolled her eyes. "Our report on England that's due Friday. Don't tell me you forgot."

"I didn't forget." He had.

"Uh-huh," she said, sounding like she didn't believe him.

Flattop buttoned the lower snaps of his jacket. "I came over here because Ms. McVey said I was really sick. I didn't want to give anyone my germs."

"Melissa Reynolds said you fell asleep in English class and woke up screaming."

Flattop cringed. Thomas Jefferson Middle School was a place where vicious rumors traveled fast. Even the true ones. "I already told you, I'm sick."

"You're not going home or anything, are you? Mrs. Penn's giving us some class time to work on our reports."

Alison Wedertz was the kind of girl who would rather

8

fall over and die in class than risk getting a *B* on anything. "I'll be there," he snapped.

"Good," she said and finally walked away. Flattop watched her join some kids on the soccer field. Once he could see that she was wrapped up in her game, he walked to the office to call his mom and go home.

Flattop trudged down the hall to Mrs. Penn's class, crumpling the excused/tardy slip in his hand. "It figures," he muttered. The one day he needed his mom to pick him up from school, she wasn't home. After wasting all of P.E. in the office, the secretary finally told him to go to Social Studies since school was almost over.

Mrs. Penn looked at both sides of the tardy slip. "Well, it looks official," she said. "Get with your report partner."

Alison stood at the back table. "Flattop! Flattop! Come on!" She waved frantically and patted a stack of books. "Look what I got at the library!" Flattop sighed, walked to the table, and flopped into a chair.

"And I have actual pictures of England," Alison said as she unfolded a Kleenex and took out five snapshots. She carefully laid them on the table. "My mom's whole family is from there."

This day would never end.

"That's Westminster Abbey," Alison said, pointing to the background of the first picture. "A lot of famous people are buried there, like the guy who wrote about Scrooge."

"Oh," was the only thing Flattop could think of to say.

"That's my mom in front. My dad let me take the picture."

There was something warm and familiar about Mrs. Wedertz's face. Flattop reached for the photograph to get a better look.

"Hold it by the edges," Alison warned. "My mom doesn't want fingerprints all over them."

Flattop gave her a sideways glance then picked up the picture by the edges. He squinted at the close-up of Alison's mom, then gasped. "Green eyes," he whispered to himself.

"What?" Alison craned her neck to look at the picture.

"Your mom has green eyes."

Alison looked at him like he was crazy. "So? About a billion people have green eyes."

Flattop leaned forward and squinted some more. Mrs. Wedertz had eyes the same color as Flattop's best cat's-eye marble. The same color as Alice's eyes.

"Give it to me," Alison ordered as she snatched the photo from his hands. "You're just trying to waste time."

Flattop could feel his ears get hot, the way they always did when he got mad. "Come on, Alison," he said, reaching for the picture again. "I've only seen one person with eyes that color."

Alison tossed her head, flipping her hair back over her shoulder. "Well, now you've seen two," she said as she tucked the picture inside her folder.

Flattop slumped in his chair and crossed his arms. "Fine."

"How're we doing back here?" Mrs. Penn asked.

"Really good," said Alison in a too-cheerful voice. "I brought in some actual pictures of England. See?"

She pointed proudly to the four remaining snapshots. "This is Wickshire. My mom's whole family is from there."

"That's exciting, Alison," Mrs. Penn said. She placed her hands on Flattop's hunched-over shoulders. "Isn't it, Flattop?"

"Can I be in a different group?" Flattop asked.

"No." Mrs. Penn's voice was icy. "Now get to work," she said as she moved to the next group.

Alison fussed with the pictures, tilting them this way and that. She picked up a snapshot of a broken-down castle. "That's the castle where my mom's family used to live a long time ago."

"That old thing?" Flattop snickered. "Haven't you ever been in a new castle?"

Alison sat up straight and pulled the picture close to her. "There's no such thing as a new castle."

"Ha!" Flattop had her now. "Yes, there is! And they have sticks and leaves on the floor called *rushes,* and candles made out of cow fat that smell like hamburgers when you burn them!"

Alison gathered up the rest of her pictures and shoved them in her folder. "They do not! They have big rugs on the floor and lights just like we have. I went there last year."

Flattop suddenly realized that it was hundreds of years ago when he stayed at Hemstead Castle. It probably looked all broken-down now, too. Here he was in a fight with Alison, and both of them were right.

He wondered if other time travelers had this problem.

When the bell rang, Flattop jumped up from his chair. "I gotta go." He went back to his desk, put on his red satin baseball jacket, grabbed his backpack, and headed for the door.

12

Alison scrambled to her feet and followed him out the door. "We haven't even done any work yet."

"The bell rang, Alison!" *Duh!* He dodged through the sea of kids on the walkway, hoping Alison would stop following him.

"Hey! Wait up!" she shouted.

Flattop hunched his shoulders and shoved his hands in his pockets, trying to ignore her.

"I'll tell Mrs. Penn you won't do your report!"

Flattop's fingers wrapped around the apple. He turned to glare at her. "You can do your report on a bunch of stupid pictures if you want. I'll do mine on *this*." He held the apple up to her face.

"An apple?"

"It's an *old* apple," he snapped. "From the Middle Ages. It may be poison, I'm not sure."

Alison took it from him and inspected it carefully. "Where'd you get it?" she asked, raising an eyebrow.

"I told you. It's from the Middle Ages."

Alison studied his face, then laughed. "Yeah. Right."

"Forget it," Flattop muttered as he turned and walked away.

"Fine!" Alison called after him. "Get an *F!* See if I care!"

Flattop didn't answer. He was too busy grumbling to himself, "Stupid report. Stupid school. Stupid Alison Wedertz." He didn't even look up when Jason and Nathan said goodbye as they rode past him on their bikes.

He was almost home when he shoved his hands back into his pockets . . . and discovered they were empty.

"Oh, great," he muttered.

His first day back in his century had been the worst

day of his life. He'd been laughed at, talked about, and now Alison Wedertz had his one and only apple.

Why had he left the Middle Ages? He had important friends there now. He'd even managed to get Margaret a one-day job at the castle. That's the kind of power he had. But here? He was a kid. A weird kid who had bad dreams in class, and had to put up with a stupid know-it-all girl who took his only proof he'd ever been in another century.

Right then and there Flattop made a decision. He was going back. Today. He took bigger strides as he made his plans. He'd go to the feast celebrating Sir William's knighthood. Then, afterward, he'd sit around and joke with green-eyed Alice until she went back to her castle in—

Flattop froze. *Wickshire?* Didn't Alison Wedertz say her mom's family was from Wickshire?

Didn't she say her mom's family used to live in a castle *a long time ago?*

And didn't Mrs. Wedertz have the same green eyes as Alice? Alice, who was about to have a baby? Flattop's stomach did a somersault. Alison Wedertz might be Alice's great-great-great-great-great—probably a thousand *greats*—granddaughter.

Flattop felt the corner of his mouth raise in a satisfied snicker. Alison Wedertz could take pictures of castles until her picture-taking finger fell off. Flattop was *friends* with her ancestors.

Flattop ran to his house as fast as he could. No doubt about it, Flattop Kincaid, Adventurer Extraordinaire, had some traveling to do.

He bolted up the steps, through the front door, and past the kitchen. He paused just long enough to see that his mother was home—finally—and busy putting away groceries.

"Hi, honey," she said. "Did you have a good—"

"Hi, Mom!" he shouted as he continued down the hall to his bedroom. "School was great, everything was great and I learned a lot of stuff and now I gotta work on my report for social studies because I want to get an *A,* so don't bother me for awhile, okay?" He stepped into his room, closed the door, and checked his watch. Three o'clock.

Flattop threw his backpack on the bed, turned on his computer and stood staring at the monitor. "Come on, come on," he said, tapping his fingers on the desk. There was the waving hand graphic, and the "Stars and Stripes Forever." Then the title:

Days and Knights
Adventures for the Third Millennium

"Let's go, Wizard. Hurry up." He looked at his watch then back at the screen. Nothing.

"I don't believe this!" he said. For the second time today, he felt his ears get hot with anger. The last thing he needed was for the Wizard to be in one of his unco-operative moods. He shrugged out of his baseball jacket.

Wait a minute! His baseball uniform! If he was going back to 1150 A.D., he had to wear what he wore the last time. He jumped up to change, muttering Coach Hartman's Red Sox dressing ceremony under his breath.

Pulling the white T-shirt with the long, red sleeves over his head, he recited, "Red sleeves mean a Red Sox player has powerful arms." Jamming his feet into tube socks, he added, "White makes my steps sure and true."

Flattop remembered William's dressing ceremony before he became a knight. *White tunic to be pure, red robe to be willing to bleed, and black cloak to remind him that he could die.* It was amazing knights weren't completely depressed by the time they got dressed in the morning.

Just thinking about William made Flattop eager to see him. He rushed through the rest of the dressing ceremony.

Stirrup socks. "Red Sox players are fast of foot."

Pants. "Red stripes mean strong legs."

Gold V-necked jersey with red satin letters that spelled RED SOX. "Red Sox players have miles-and-miles-and-miles of heart."

Red cap. "A Red Sox player outthinks opponents."

Finally, he pulled on his baseball cleats, tightened and double-knotted the laces, then shoved his arms into the sleeves of his jacket and sat down at the computer.

"Okay, Wizard," he said. "Let's go."

Nothing.

He pounded his fists on the desk. Had he forgotten anything? He looked down at his uniform and—

"The glass!" He needed the thick, purple-y black rectangle of glass that came with the game. He rummaged through his desk drawer. "Found it!" he said, raising the dark glass triumphantly.

"Bravo, my boy!" came the familiar voice from the computer speakers.

Flattop looked at the monitor and saw the Wizard, dressed in his purple robe and pointy hat. "It's about time you showed up," Flattop scolded.

"It's about time you remembered your traveling

clothes, my boy. Goodness sakes, we can't have you suddenly popping back into Lord Hemstead's castle in different clothes, can we? I mean, what would people think?'' The Wizard chuckled and smoothed the hair at the tip of his long, white beard. ''Imagine the fuss that would create. Oh, my. It would never do.''

''Can we go now?'' Flattop realized he sounded rude the minute he said it. ''Please?'' he added.

The Wizard sighed. ''You know, I'm beginning to believe the art of conversation is dead. But, very well, Marvin. You know the rules. Once we're back in 1150 A.D., you must catch me in human form, touch the dark glass to my hand, and—''

''I win. I get to come home. Let's go.''

The Wizard raised his hand toward Flattop until a close-up of his palm filled the entire screen.

Flattop took a deep breath and touched the dark glass to the monitor.

Purple lightning flashes streaked through his brain. Even though he'd seen them before, they were still scary. His heartbeat grew stronger, louder, faster, until he was afraid his eardrums would burst. *There's gotta be a way to make this time travel thing a little easier to take,* he thought.

Then everything went black.

3

"Flattop? Flattop? Can you hear me?" A woman's voice called to him from deep inside his brain. Flattop's eyelids felt like they weighed a ton as he struggled to open them.

"He is awakening," the voice said. "Margaret, fetch me some water, please."

"Yes, m'lady."

Flattop squinted, trying his best to focus on the figure that leaned over him. But all he could see was a fuzzy confusion of black and white.

"Rest, lad," the voice said.

The image before Flattop blurred, doubled, then finally came into focus. He looked into the familiar green eyes. "Alice," he said, smiling. "It's you."

"Yes, 'tis me," she said, a concerned look on her face.

"You didn't have your baby yet?"

Alice blushed bright red and laid her hand on her bulging stomach. "Goodness, no!"

"Oh. I just wondered. I hadn't seen you for awhile and—" He stopped, trying to find a way to finish the sentence. "You know . . . for awhile."

Alice smiled. "You gave us quite a fright."

"I did?" Flattop looked around. He'd expected to come back to the Middle Ages in the same place he'd left them. But he wasn't in the cobblestone alley where he'd crashed into the Wizard and then gone home. Instead, he was in his chamber in Hemstead Castle, on the down mattress in the four-poster bed. "I thought I'd be lying in the street."

"Goodness, boy, you *were*." Alice felt his forehead. "Margaret found you and alerted me. We had you carried here to the donjon."

Flattop smiled, pleased he recognized the word. The donjon was the safest tower in the castle. It not only stored the grain and farming supplies, it held the Great Hall and all of the bedrooms. He'd only been in this century a few minutes and he already felt more comfortable than he did at home.

Alice patted his hand. "I hope you are convinced now that apples cannot be eaten uncooked."

"Huh?" Now he was confused again.

"Margaret saw you fetch an apple from the kitchen. When we found you lying on the ground, the apple was gone." Alice felt his forehead. "It did not take us long to figure out that you ate it."

"But I . . ." Flattop decided not to argue with her. "You're right. I should've listened to your advice," he said, trying to look ashamed.

Margaret ran into the room carrying a wooden bowl of water and a piece of cloth. She handed them to Alice, then smiled at Flattop. "Are you feeling better?"

"Yeah," he answered, then added, "I ate an apple."

Alice soaked the cloth with water, then wiped off Flattop's face. "I warrant he will never do it again."

"Nope." He smiled at Margaret. "So, how do you like working here?"

Margaret beamed. She stepped closer to the bed and whispered, "Lady Hemstead says I have proven myself. She says I may continue to work in the castle."

"Cool!" Flattop whispered back.

"I shall have first pickings from the scraps in the cookhouse, just as the other servants do." Margaret blushed, then smiled at Flattop. "My family thanks you for your kind help."

Flattop felt a warm, glowing sensation fill his chest. For the first time, he had made a difference in somebody's life. Grown-ups were always making a difference—giving money to charity, recycling, saving animals from becoming extinct. Maybe this good feeling was why they did it.

Alice bent over and tucked a stray wisp of Margaret's hair back in her yellow scarf. "Let him rest now," she said softly.

"Aye, m'lady." Margaret stood, curtsied to Flattop, then to Alice, and scurried out the door.

Pleased with his good deed, Flattop put his hands behind his head and sighed.

Alice tightened the strips of red fabric tied to each of the four wooden bedposts.

"What're those?" he asked.

"'Tis red cloth to help you recover," Alice said as she wiped his face again. "Goodness, lad. Do you know nothing of modern medicine?"

Flattop shrugged. "I guess not."

"Red fights the effects of the poison. It balances the body and restores it to health. Everyone knows that."

Flattop had never heard anything so silly in his life. "Where's William?" he asked.

"He is celebrating in the Great Hall," Alice answered.

The party! Flattop sat straight up in bed. He'd come back to the Middle Ages to go to William's feast, and here he was wasting time pretending to be poisoned. He scrambled to his feet. "I gotta go!" He started for the door, then motioned to Alice. "Come on, we're missing everything!"

"But you are ailing," she argued. "You must rest."

"I'm okay now," he said. "It must be those red things on the bedposts." He surprised himself with how fast he'd come up with that answer. He motioned for her once more. "Come on, let's go!"

He opened the door for Alice, and the two of them hurried through the stone-walled corridor, down the steps, and into the Great Hall.

The musicians were playing a lively tune and a group of people, including Lord and Lady Hemstead, were holding hands and dancing in a circle. Others stood around talking and laughing. Smells of roasted ham, onion, and garlic made Flattop's stomach growl. He'd skipped lunch at school and left his house before dinner. Now he was starving.

He tugged on the sleeve of his jacket and sneaked a peek at his watch. Noon. He'd never noticed that time travel automatically adjusted his watch. He was roused out of his thoughts by a strong slap on the back. He turned around to see William's smiling face.

"Flattop! Welcome!" he shouted. "'Tis good to see you have recovered from your illness."

"I ate an apple," Flattop announced.

William laughed and slapped Flattop's back again. "So I understand. I hope you have learned a valuable lesson this day."

"Yeah," he nodded, wishing they'd found an explanation that made him look less stupid.

"Come, my friend," William said. "We shall fill your gullet with good food." William guided him over to the head table and sat him in a high-backed chair. Flattop could feel his stomach rumble in anticipation.

William picked up a wooden plate that had leftover food stuck to it and brushed the scraps onto the floor with one swipe of his hand. Then he reached into the gaping hole on the side of a roasted pig, pulled a handful of meat off the bones, and deposited it on the plate. After he licked his fingers and the palm of his hand, William tore off a chunk of bread, piled it on top of the meat, and smiled at Flattop.

Flattop did his best to smile back.

"We must not forget the best part," William said, as he reached into a bowl of gooey, honey-covered cooked pears and plopped two on Flattop's plate. "There," he said proudly, as he put the plate in front of Flattop. "A feast for a king."

"Thanks," Flattop said weakly.

" 'Tis my pleasure, friend."

Flattop smiled. *Friend.* For the first time today he felt he really belonged.

Sir Humphrey walked over and clamped his hand on Flattop's shoulder. "Well, lad, what do you think of our new knight?"

"I think he's pretty cool," said Flattop.

"Aye," Sir Humphrey said, winking at William. "I know a lady or two who share your high opinion." William blushed bright red and shook his head. Humphrey laughed and pulled William away from the table toward a group of ladies in long, colorful tunics.

Knights, Flattop thought. *What a bunch of great guys.*

He tore a chunk of roast pig off the handful William had given him, then noticed the head of the pig was staring at him from its place on the table. Flattop turned away and popped the chunk of meat in his mouth. But when he tried to chew it, the image of the pig's head haunted him.

Finally, hunger won out, and he discovered that if he closed his eyes and pictured his baseball team posed in front of the dugout at the Little League field, he could eat his food without wanting to spit it out all over the floor.

Just as Flattop was taking his last bite of bread, he felt a nudge under the table. It was the black-and-brown dog who had befriended him during his first trip.

"Hey, Brutus!" Flattop smiled, scratching the dog under the chin. "Haven't seen you in awhile." Brutus pushed his nose into Flattop's hand. Flattop bent down to nuzzle the dog, but a glimpse into the dog's eyes stopped him. An unmistakable, undoglike wisdom shone through, which meant the Wizard had decided to use Brutus's body for a hiding place, not for the first time.

"Wizard! It's you!" Flattop whispered.

The dog opened its mouth in a wide, panting smile.

Flattop laughed. It was good to be back . . . in his game.

......

4

Flattop rolled over in the big bed and nudged something with his foot. Brutus.

Everyone had looked at Flattop like he was crazy when he insisted Brutus sleep on the bed. William was especially unhappy, since there was barely enough room for the two of them without a big dog stretched out in the middle. But the Wizard was Flattop's ticket home. Even if things were going well, he felt better with the Wizard close at hand.

He studied the snoring lump on the other side of the bed. The dog-on-the-bed issue didn't seem to bother William now. Flattop checked his watch. Four o'clock in the morning. He rubbed his finger over the black wrist band. The watch was a birthday present from his grandfather. Normally, he'd show it off, but he knew a high-tech, shock-proof, water-proof, digital sports watch could be mistaken for witchcraft and get him killed. It was best to keep it a secret. He pushed the band up his arm as far as it would go, then pulled his jacket sleeve over it. No one seemed to care about his weird-looking clothes. To them he was a rich noble from a land called California . . . which was located somewhere in France.

Sitting up, he looked into the dog's eyes. The Wizard

was still there. Brutus slurped a big, wet kiss across Flattop's face, then jumped off the bed and scratched at the door. Flattop opened it to see Alice walking down the corridor.

Startled, she gasped, then backed up against the wall, with one hand holding a flickering candle, the other resting on her stomach.

"Alice," Flattop said in a low whisper. "It's me."

Alice held the candle up to his face. "Flattop! What are you doing awake?"

"I was going to ask you the same thing."

Alice laughed softly. "I must leave for Wickshire. The wagon is waiting to take me home."

It was as though she'd said she was taking the sun out of the sky. "Why?" he asked.

"My husband needs me," she said. "And my babe will come soon."

Flattop remembered the night he'd helped her walk to her bedchamber. He'd thought she was going to have her baby then and there. Maybe she *should* go home, where her husband could take care of her. Where her doctor was.

"Okay," was all he could say.

"You shall follow later today," she said, her green eyes twinkling.

"I . . . shall?"

"My husband has sent for both you and William." Alice smoothed the fabric of her black-and-white dress with her hand. "He has scheduled a tournament in honor of his brother's dubbing. After that, William shall make his home with us in Wickshire Castle."

"Oh." Flattop stared at the floor, wondering where he fit into all these plans.

Alice took his hand. "And you, lad, are free to stay with us as long as you wish."

Flattop looked up to see her smiling. "Thanks, Alice," he said. The big lump in his throat stopped him from saying anything else. So he kissed her hand, like he'd done the first time he'd met her. And she laughed out loud.

Holding her arm, Flattop carefully led her through the narrow corridors, past the bedchambers, then down the stone steps and through the Great Hall. He held the candle and walked in front of Alice to light the way down the wooden stairs that wound around the outside of the donjon.

At the bottom, two servants helped her into a horse-drawn wagon. The driver slapped the reins and the horses started pulling across the inner, then the outer drawbridge.

"Drive carefully," Flattop said, waving good-bye. He listened to the wagon creak and clunk, and Alice and the driver bounced and shook over every bump. Too bad they didn't have a car with really good shocks like the one Jason's dad owned.

When he turned to go back up the donjon steps, he almost tripped over Brutus. He scratched behind the dog's ears and whispered to the Wizard, "She's a nice lady, isn't she, Bru—" Flattop looked into the dog's eyes. They were just dog's eyes again.

The Wizard was gone.

Flattop sighed. He suddenly felt very alone.

He patted Brutus on the head. "Come on, boy." They walked back up to the bedchamber and went back to sleep.

Flattop awoke to a faint clinking sound next to him on the bed. He raised his head and opened his eyes. William was gone.

One of the servants, a boy about Flattop's age, was smoothing out chain mail on the empty side of the bed. He bowed quickly. "Forgive me. Sir William said you would not mind."

Flattop's gaze scanned the room for the black-and-brown dog. "Where's Brutus?"

"He ran out the door as I entered. I am certain you will find him begging scraps at the cookhouse door." The servant continued to tug at the metal-link tunic.

"What're you doing?" Flattop asked.

"I was summoned to prepare Sir William for his journey home."

"Good morning, Flattop," William said as he stepped in from the adjoining room, wrapped in a sheet and rubbing his wet hair with a corner of the fabric. "Your bath is ready."

Flattop shuddered. William had beaten him to the clean bath water like he always did.

"Flattop?" William waved his hands in front of Flattop's face.

"Yeah, yeah," Flattop grumbled. "I guess I'm just tired."

"Sloth is a sin, my friend," William said as he tugged on the gray pants that looked like a cross between sweater sleeves and baggy tights.

"Sloth?"

"Laziness. 'Tis a sin. One must work hard to enjoy the riches of heaven."

"Yeah, well, I helped Alice get to her wagon while you were in here snoring, so I'm not that lazy," Flattop answered in defense.

"How gallant, my friend." William smiled mischievously.

He was teasing. Flattop felt like an idiot for taking it

seriously—the way his four-year-old cousin did when Flattop called him a baby.

Flattop watched William pull on his soft leather shoes that flopped around like socks. He wondered if he should apologize for acting like a four-year-old.

To Flattop's relief, William dropped the whole subject of *sloth*. "To show his gratitude for dispatching the Robber King, Lord Hemstead has gifted us with a bag of gold and our choice of two horses from the villain's stock. I have chosen the large gelding ridden by the Robber King." William stood up and walked toward the door. "Do you have a preference as to your mount, or shall I make the choice for you?"

Flattop needed a moment for his brain to process words like *gelding* and *mount*.

"Flattop?" William pressed for an answer.

Flattop pretended to know what he was talking about. "I'll take a gelding or a mount or whatever you think would be good."

William nodded, but he looked confused. He opened the door, then looked back at Flattop. "You *do* know how to ride a horse . . ."

Flattop forced a laugh. "Of course I do."

William smiled and left the chamber, closing the big wooden door behind him.

Flattop shrugged. "How hard could it be?"

5

"Auuggghhh!" Flattop bent over the front of his run-away horse as it galloped into Hemstead Forest at lightning speed. He clutched its mane with whitened fists and screamed, "Help!" Low-slung tree limbs slapped the top of his head and scraped along his back. "Somebody help me, please!" Flattop closed his eyes and pushed his head against the horse's massive neck.

It seemed like hours before a steadying hand reached underneath his chest, grabbed the reins, and pulled back on them. When the horse finally slowed to a stop, Flattop looked up to see William frowning. "I thought you said you could ride."

"I can," Flattop answered, remembering all the pony rides he'd been on. "It's just that—this horse is different."

The instant William handed the reins to Flattop, the horse reared up on its hind legs. Flattop felt the high wooden back of the saddle dig into his spine. "Get me off this thing!"

"Drop the reins and lean over the horse's head. Hold onto his mane," William coached.

"Make up your mind!" Flattop shouted as he dropped the reins. With one big push, he stretched over the horse's neck. The horse lowered his head and stood still. Flattop heaved a sigh of relief and relaxed. "Finally."

"You have a spirited mount. You must push your knees into his sides to show him who is master."

With one hand tangled in the horse's mane, Flattop reached for the reins with the other. He slowly, carefully sat up. The horse raised its head and shook its mane. "Your knees! Show him who is master!" William repeated.

Flattop pushed his knees hard into the horse's giant barrel chest.

Almost as if by magic, the horse seemed to calm down.

William tilted his head to one side and asked, "Do you not know how to handle horses?"

"Not when they act crazy and run all over the place," Flattop complained.

"I should think your training as a noble would have included extensive horsemanship," William said.

"Yeah, well, we don't ride horses very much in California."

William's eyes grew wide with surprise. "Then how do you travel?"

Flattop looked away and grimaced. He couldn't tell William about cars, trains, and airplanes. "We just . . . ride around in . . . wagons." Relief washed over him. When he'd started that sentence, he had no idea how he'd finish it.

William shook his head and trotted out in front of Flattop. "Very well," he said. "Let us be on our way."

It seemed like days later when Flattop pulled up the sleeve of his jacket to sneak a peek at his watch. They'd been riding for almost three hours, mostly in silence.

William rode about twenty yards ahead, looking relaxed as he gazed at the countryside. Flattop was bored—and sore. He gritted his teeth and shifted his weight in the saddle. When he was a little kid, he thought it would be great to be a cowboy. Now he wasn't so sure. Every inch of his body ached.

"Hey, William! When are we gonna be there?"

William scanned the horizon, studied the position of the sun in the sky and said, "Soon."

Flattop heaved a disgusted sigh. *Soon.* That's what his dad always said. He pulled his shoulders back to stretch his chest muscles. It felt like he'd been punched about a hundred times. He was sure there were bruises under his shirt.

He let his head droop forward to ease the stiffness in his neck, then bent at the waist to stretch his lower back. When his ribs hit the front of the saddle, he felt a dull, aching pain. Leaning over to hang on to his galloping, runaway horse had pounded the saddle into his chest with every step.

He slowly sat up and shifted his weight again. "Hey William. How long have you been riding horses?"

William slowed his horse, allowing Flattop to catch up. As they rode side by side, William looked into the sky as though he was in deep thought. "I recall riding with my father, Lord Wickshire, before I was fostered out to Hemstead."

"I thought your brother was Lord Wickshire."

William tilted his head and studied Flattop. "Are you not familiar with peerage?"

Flattop looked down and clenched the reins a little tighter. His mind raced through all the words he knew. *Peerage.* Finally he shrugged and said, "I know *porridge.*"

William raised his eyebrow and chuckled. The chuckle grew into a laugh. Then into a big laugh. "Porridge!" he repeated, laughing some more.

Flattop scowled and looked away. *Peerage,* he thought. *Stupid word. Who cares what it means?*

Finally, William shook his head and sighed. "Ah, my friend, you have a ready wit," he said as he wiped his eyes. "You are surely the toast of any court."

"Yeah. Pretty much," Flattop said, though he had no idea what William was talking about.

"It is likely that you use a different word in California. *Peerage* is the rank and title of our nobles. When my father was alive, he was the Lord of Wickshire Castle and all the surrounding lands, so he was called 'Lord Wickshire.' When he died, the title of Lord Wickshire was handed down to my brother, James, since he was the oldest son."

"You mean like when a king dies and the queen gets to run everything?"

William gasped. "My heavens, no! The title and the lands are passed to the eldest son. Women cannot be given that kind of responsibility."

"Why not?" Flattop asked.

William looked at Flattop as though he had just asked the dumbest question in the world. "Women cannot lead armies or handle weapons. They are not capable of making important decisions concerning the land and the people. God did not create them for such a purpose."

Miss Know-It-All Alison Wedertz would probably kick William in the shins for saying that, Flattop thought. "Then what *is* their purpose?" he asked.

William sat up in his saddle and looked like he was about to give a speech or sing a song or something. "Women were created to inspire men. They are the reason men fight bravely in battle. Women serve their men, tend to the home, and give us strong, healthy sons to manage our land.''

Flattop looked at the green hillsides and thought about the women back in his century who flew planes, fired guns, and went to war—not to mention the ones who were leaders of whole countries. Flattop thought about telling him that, then decided William would be so shocked he'd probably fall off his horse.

William pulled out ahead of Flattop again, as though he was some kind of big, important general and Flattop was just a little kid tagging along.

Flattop frowned. Maybe becoming a knight had made *Sir* William a little stuck-up. Flattop did his best to shrug it off. It wouldn't be long before he'd be at Wickshire Castle. Then he'd see Alice again. *She* didn't have a conceited bone in her body, even though she was *Lady* Wickshire.

Just as the sun set, William paused at the top of a grassy hill. He motioned for Flattop to join him. Below lay a cluster of buildings surrounded by a tall, wooden fence. It reminded him of the condos his grandmother lived in—where kids could only swim in the pool from ten o'clock until noon.

''The alehouse is in that town,'' William said. He looked over his shoulder at the setting sun. ''We shall spend the night there, then be on our way tomorrow.''

''Sure,'' Flattop agreed. ''No problem.'' This would be like staying in a motel when his family went on vacation.

William spurred his horse and trotted out in front of Flattop—again.

Flattop rolled his eyes and heaved a disgusted sigh, then followed *Sir* William down the hill.

6

"How far away is your castle?" Flattop asked as they rode to the open wooden gates of the town.

"*Lord Wickshire's* castle is almost a day's ride hence," William said.

Flattop nudged the brim of his baseball cap a little farther up on his forehead. "If your mom and dad owned your family's castle, don't you own part of it now?"

"Goodness, no," William answered. "Lord Wickshire owns the castle."

"But, Lord Wick—*James* is your brother. Won't he share it with you?"

"I am but his guest and, for as long as he will have me, his humble and grateful servant."

It sounded more like William was going to work for a new boss than going home to be with his family. If Flattop had been away from his home for ten years, he'd probably spend a whole day hugging everybody. Even his sister, Marcia.

A terrible thought crossed his mind. What if he had to go home and be Marcia's humble and grateful servant? He could see her lying on the bed talking to her boyfriend-of-the-week while Flattop cleaned her room or painted her toenails or something.

William led Flattop through the tall, wooden gates and down the narrow cobblestone street. This place definitely wasn't like his grandmother's condo. Two-story buildings were jammed together. The top floors were bigger than the bottom ones, and they looked like they'd tip over in a stiff breeze. The narrow alleys between were barely walkways.

Piles of garbage lay on the sides of the streets and pigs nosed through the food scraps. On top of one pile, two dogs fought over a bone.

A heavy, rotting smell hung in the air. It made Flattop think of the garbage dump that his parents drove by once in awhile. He always tried to hold his breath until they were past it. But this whole town stunk. He tried breathing through his mouth, but the disgusting odor seemed to penetrate through his taste buds and go to his brain anyway.

William glanced over his shoulder at Flattop. "We shall stable our horses at the livery then get some supper and a room at the alehouse."

"Uh huh," Flattop said, the stench making his eyes water.

As they handed their horses to the livery man, Flattop took in a deep breath of stable air. It smelled of dust, hay, and horses—which was like fancy perfume compared to the streets. He thought about asking if he could sleep in the stable, but decided he'd better do what *Sir* William wanted. Flattop filled his lungs one last time, then walked into the rancid afternoon air.

On each side of the street, Flattop noticed shallow, stone-lined trenches that were about five times bigger than the rain gutters on his house. *Must be for rain,* he thought. He wondered if someone had to rake the leaves out of it the way he had to at home.

Hearing a click, he looked into one of the tiny walkways between the buildings. A woman opened a second-story window and emptied a chamber pot onto the walkway below. Flattop watched the contents flow down to the street, into the gutter, and past his feet. It had never occurred to him where everything went when he flushed the toilet at home, but he was glad it didn't float down the street for everyone to see.

"Flattop," William called out. "Come."

Flattop backed away from the gutter and hurried after William.

They opened the wooden door to the Hart's Blood Inn and stepped inside. Flattop had seen movies where guys went to inns and got in fights. He looked forward to seeing people sword fighting, falling off balconies, and swinging from chandeliers. But there were no chandeliers in the Hart's Blood Inn. The ceiling was too low to swing on anything without looking stupid.

He counted ten heavy, wooden tables like he'd seen in the Great Hall at Hemstead Castle. On one side of the room, a bunch of ladies talked and giggled. On the other side, the men sat huddled in conversation, then laughed loudly and slapped each other on the back.

Flattop remembered his first after-school dance in the sixth grade, where the girls stayed on one side of the cafeteria and the boys stayed on the other. It looked like things hadn't changed much in hundreds of years.

People on both sides of the room turned to look at William and Flattop as they entered.

William stood at attention. "Greetings," he said. "I am called Sir William, recently of Hemstead. This is my traveling companion, Flattop Kincaid, a noble from the land of California. We seek food and lodging before continuing our journey to Wickshire Castle, where I shall serve my brother James, Lord Wickshire.''

"Enough said, good sir,'' came a husky, female voice from the back of the room. "Sit yourself down and I shall fetch each of you a tankard of ale.''

Flattop stood at the door, his gaze searching the shadows for the woman. In the next instant, he realized William had taken a seat at a table crowded with scruffy men. They were clasping hands and making introductions.

Flattop stood alone at the door and nervously drummed his fingers on his thighs. He was suddenly aware that all the women were looking at him and whispering. He turned his back and checked to make sure the zipper on his pants was pulled up. It was.

When he heard the women giggle, he turned around and walked as fast as he could to William's table, squeezing between William and another man.

"Flattop,'' William said, with a slap on the back. "I'd like you to meet George the Miller, Richard the Weaver and . . .'' His voice trailed off, a signal for the next man to state his name.

"Charles Baker,'' said the man.

"Henry Shoemaker,'' said the next.

"Robert Butcher.''

"Harold Carpenter.''

Flattop listened carefully to the names, then smiled, delighted to have discovered something new. In a time when no one seemed to have a last name but him, he found a whole group of men who'd turned their jobs— *miller, weaver, baker, shoemaker, butcher, carpenter*— into last names.

Flattop held out his hand. "Pleased to meet you Mr. Miller, Mr. Weaver, Mr.—''

The men withdrew their hands and eyed him suspiciously.

"Flattop," William said, "these are tradesmen. Nobles do not address commoners as *mister*. They think you are mocking them."

Flattop felt his face turn hot with embarrassment. Couldn't he do *anything* right? "I—I'm sorry. Where I come from, we have to call adults 'mister' and 'miss' and—"

"The boy meant no offense," William said, interrupting.

"Since when did this sorry lot of gents become so soft?" came the woman's voice Flattop had heard earlier. A powerful arm reached past him to set a tankard of ale in front of William and another in front of Flattop. "Drink up, boy," the voice said to Flattop.

He turned around to see a huge female figure in a dark blue tunic, with a long, dark blue scarf wrapped around her head, under her chin, and across her throat. Her face was dusted with a white powder that made her look a little like a ghost. Flattop knew it was impolite to stare, but he couldn't help himself. "Thanks," he said, then pulled the tankard of ale closer.

The woman bent down and half-whispered in his ear, "If these fools give you any trouble, lad, you call for old Blanche."

Charles Baker laughed. "Aye! Blanche will give you all the trouble you need!" The men roared with laughter and pounded on the table.

Blanche acted like she was insulted, then shouted, " 'Tis true!" and laughed as hard as the rest of them. "Sit tight," she yelled over her shoulder as she disappeared into the shadows at the back of the inn. "I shall bring you some supper."

Flattop sipped the brown ale. It tasted like really strong apple cider and made his lips pucker. But after a couple more swallows, he got used to it.

In a matter of minutes, Flattop and William were staring at two plates piled high with Blanche's homemade sausages and cooked cabbage. Flattop picked up a sausage and bit into it. It was good. In fact, it tasted better than the sausage he ate at home. He wondered what Blanche put in it to make it taste so good.

After they'd eaten, William began to tell the story of the evil Robber King of Hemstead Forest and how he had killed the "foul villain." But he wasn't just telling the story, he was acting it out.

Overacting.

He stood up and gestured broadly at all the big, dramatic parts. Everyone in the alehouse listened, wide-eyed.

Flattop felt the world getting a little fuzzy and he struggled to keep his eyes open. William hadn't even gotten to the exciting part yet. Flattop stifled a yawn. Feeling a tap on his shoulder, he turned around to see Blanche motioning for him to come with her. He got up and followed her to a narrow, wooden staircase.

"You look tired, lad, and your knight will be telling his stories for a while longer yet," she whispered. "Let me show you to your room." Blanche held a candle to light the way and led Flattop up the stairs.

"I don't know what's the matter with William," Flattop said. "He usually doesn't talk this much."

Blanche chuckled. "Nonsense, boy. He is a knight. 'Tis his duty to entertain us with stories of his glorious battles." She opened the door to one of the bedrooms and led Flattop inside.

The bed was smaller than the one at Hemstead, and

the covers looked more like horse blankets, but Flattop was tired. A bed was a bed, as far as he was concerned. A straight-backed wooden chair stood in one corner. Next to it was a chamber pot and a pile of straw. *Not again,* Flattop sighed to himself.

Chamber pots were a necessity for all people except the serfs. *They* went to the bathroom outside—in rivers, behind bushes, anywhere. But everyone else used a chamber pot.

Blanche set the candle in a holder and Flattop watched it flicker as the draft from the open window teased the flame. "Sleep well, lad," she said and started for the door.

Flattop suddenly remembered that he and William hadn't paid for dinner or their room. "Wait! Blanche! I don't have any money but William does and—"

"Hush now," she said, smiling. "I am pleased to offer my hospitality to anyone who is kin to Lady Wickshire."

Flattop's mouth dropped open. "You know Alice?"

"Aye, and a finer woman 'twas never born," she said. "When my husband took ill five winters ago, 'twas Alice who tended to his fever. And when he died, she made me a loan to keep the alehouse running."

"She's a friend of mine," Flattop said proudly, then wondered if it was okay to say that about a married woman who was a noble. "I mean, you know, a . . . friend." He shrugged his shoulders, unable to come up with a better word.

"Aye, lad, that she is." Blanche patted Flattop on the shoulder, then headed for the stairs.

7

"Cover fire!" a man's voice rang out in the stillness of the night.

Flattop opened his eyes and rolled onto his back, hearing the straw mattress underneath him crackle and crunch.

"Cover fire!" the voice from the street shouted again.

The door opened and Flattop propped himself up on his elbows to see William stagger in, holding a candle. "Is there a fire?" Flattop asked.

"No," William said, pulling off his tunic. "It's curfew. Time for everyone to cover their hearth fires and go to bed." He bent down and pulled the chain mail over his head. It hit the wooden floor like a sack of coins. William groaned and raked his hand through his dark hair. "I fear I have drunk too much ale this night." He blew out the candle and crawled into bed, pulling the covers over his shoulders.

Maybe that's why Flattop had gotten tired so fast. The ale tasted like strong apple cider but it had the same effect as a cold medicine he'd taken one time.

William sighed and began to breathe slower and deeper.

"Cover fire!" the voice was farther away now.

"William?"

"Hmmm?"

"Who's that guy out there?" Flattop asked.

"He's the watchman. He patrols the streets."

"You mean like 'Ten o'clock and all's well'?" Flattop had heard that in a movie once.

"Hmmm?"

"You know . . . he makes sure nobody attacks or anything," Flattop explained.

"No." William sounded a little impatient. "I told you, he *is* a watchman. He watches for fires."

"Fires?"

"Aye. Even a small cook fire can quickly grow and destroy a town like this in the blink of an eye."

"Oh." Flattop thought about the fire engines he had in his century. And fire extinguishers and smoke alarms and phones to call for help. A little town in the middle of nowhere in the year 1150 A.D. could be wiped out "in the blink of an eye."

"Cover fire!" The voice could barely be heard.

Flattop wondered why people would choose to live in a town. Why didn't they live inside castle walls like the bakers and livery men in Hemstead? Even serfs like John and Ruth had a better life than this. They didn't have to live all jammed together with piles of rotting garbage in the streets.

"William?"

"Flattop, please," William said. "Go to sleep."

Flattop lay quietly, staring into the darkness. Tomorrow they'd be at Wickshire Castle and he'd see Alice again. Maybe she'd had her baby. If nobles had feasts just because a guy became a knight, he could imagine what kind of celebration they'd have when a baby was born.

William's breathing turned into snoring. Flattop sighed. He rolled away from William, raised his watch to his face, and pushed the button to light the dial.

Nine-thirty. *And all's well.*

The next morning, after a breakfast of Blanche's homemade, boiled sausages and baked apples, William and Flattop were on their way, with William in the lead, as usual.

"Give Lady Wickshire my best regards!" Blanche called to them as they rode down the street and through the open gates.

"Fear not, good woman," William called back. "We shall deliver your message."

"Yeah," Flattop added. "We'll tell her *hi* for you."

About a half hour later, they crested the second hill of that morning. William waited for Flattop to join him and they both looked down at two large wood-and-stone buildings, separated by tall fences and surrounded by rich, green farmland. Flattop searched the landscape for a castle, but there wasn't any.

"So . . . is this Wickshire?" Flattop tried not to sound disappointed, but it sure didn't look anything like Alison Wedertz's pictures.

William laughed. "My little friend, *all* of this land is Wickshire!"

Flattop wondered when he'd become William's "little" friend.

"My brother oversees and protects the town where we stayed last night as well as the monastery and convent below."

"A convent? With nuns?"

"Aye." William nodded.

"And a monastery with monks and everything?"

"Aye," William said with a smile.

"Cool!" Flattop had seen nuns before, but the only monk he'd ever seen was Friar Tuck in a Robin Hood movie. He squinted at the beige buildings with dark brown roofs, straining to see details. Both were designed like two-story apartment buildings with courtyards in the center.

"Come," William said, nudging his horse forward. "We shall pay a visit to the good brothers."

Flattop nudged his heels into his horse's belly and followed. "Do you think they'll let us?"

"I am certain of it. My father, Lord Wickshire, bestowed many gifts on the Benedictine brothers and granted many favors to the abbot. As his son, I am always welcome." William looked over his shoulder and winked mischievously at Flattop. "Besides, my younger brother is one of the monks."

Flattop gasped. "You're kidding! You've got a brother who's a—a—brother?"

"Aye."

As they rode through the fields, Flattop saw men in long brown robes tending the crops. For the first time since he'd been in the Middle Ages, the movies had gotten something right—these monks were dressed like Friar Tuck. The only difference was that they wore big, floppy brown hoods that shaded most of their faces.

Unlike the town's thick, wooden gate, the monastery had iron railings like the kind Flattop had seen in front of rich people's houses—or jails. As they approached the closed gate, one of the monks walked forward to greet them.

William sat up straight in his saddle. "I am William of Wickshire. My friend and I have come seeking my brother, Quentin."

The figure nodded, then unhooked and opened the gate. "Brother Quentin is in the cloisters. You may pass through the chapel," the monk said softly.

William dismounted and led his horse toward the stables at the side of the big building. Flattop jumped off his horse right in front of the monk. Peering at the shadowed face surrounded by the brown hood, he said, "Thanks for opening the gate and everything."

"You are welcome, lad," the voice replied.

Flattop tugged on his horse's reins to catch up with William. All around him, monks worked quietly. Some tended the garden along the building. Others replaced stones that had fallen out of the fence.

In the first stalls, pigs grunted and rolled in the mud. In the next, several monks were prodding cows out to graze. Inside the third stable, they found a boy who looked younger than Flattop, but was also in a brown, hooded robe. He stopped raking through the horse stalls and, without saying a word, took the reins from William and Flattop.

Flattop tagged along behind William as he headed for the chapel. "How old is your brother?"

"Quentin has seen fourteen winters."

Fourteen years old and already a monk. Of course, William was only seventeen and he was already a knight. "You sure have to grow up fast around here," he whispered to himself.

Flattop tried to imagine what it would be like to live a half day's ride from the nearest town. "How come they built the monastery all the way out here?" asked Flattop.

"Brothers of the Benedictine order have chosen to live apart from the distractions of our modern society." William entered the chapel and quietly walked across the room. When Flattop tried to follow, his baseball cleats rattled on the stone floor. William glared at him. Flattop froze in place until the echo stopped, then walked on tiptoe to the other side of the room.

"What do monks do all day?" Flattop whispered.

"They lead a life of prayer, hard work, and quiet contemplation," William said as he opened the door on the other side of the chapel.

"Look out!" shouted the voice of a young man.

A ball bounced off the top of the open door and a brown-robed body slammed into William, knocking him down.

The monk, who looked like a teenager, quickly stood up and offered his hand to William. "Forgive me, good sir. I was not watching where—" He squinted into the knight's face. "William?"

William looked at the young man, then laughed and shouted, "Quentin!"

Flattop stood in the chapel doorway while William and Quentin hollered and hugged, then took turns picking each other up. So much for the quiet life of a monk.

William beamed at his brother. "You have grown taller!"

Quentin slapped William's stomach. "You have grown fatter!"

"Careful how you treat me," William said, laughing. "I am *Sir* William now."

Quentin pushed him away playfully. "How is it that they have dubbed a lackwit like you?"

They alternated giving each other headlocks and begging for mercy.

Flattop smiled. Somehow, this was what he thought should happen when two brothers met after a long time. Too bad Flattop didn't have a brother. Marcia would never understand a glad-to-see-you headlock.

William put an arm around Flattop's shoulder and pulled him into the reunion. "Quentin. I would like you to meet Flattop Kincaid. He is a noble from the land of California!"

"California?" Quentin asked. "I am not familiar with California."

Deciding to stick to the same story he'd told everyone

in Hemstead, Flattop said, "It's in France." He forced a smile. He'd just lied to a monk.

"I am quite familiar with France," Quentin stated. "We have transcribed books and maps of the region. Perhaps you can show me where your California is."

Flattop could feel beads of sweat break out on his upper lip. "Uh . . . yeah . . . perhaps I could." He glanced at William then back at Quentin. "Of course, we probably have to get going pretty soon. We don't want to keep Lord Wickshire waiting, do we Wil—"

William had picked up the ball and crossed the court-yard to a group of young monks. Flattop sighed. He was out of lies. He shrugged. Maybe lightning could strike him dead. Maybe space aliens could take him away. Or maybe the Wizard would show up and zap him home.

"Quentin!" William shouted. "How does one play this game?"

Quentin turned and walked toward his brother. "It is very simple . . . for *most* of us!"

The subject was changed! Flattop felt a wave of relief wash over him. "Thank you," he whispered to Whoever might be listening.

Quentin began instructing William in what seemed to be a basic game of handball. "You must hit the ball with the palm of your hand so that it strikes the wall. Then your opponent must try to return it in the same manner." Quentin motioned for one of the monks to join him. "Brother Mark?"

Mark nodded, stepped forward, and smacked the ball into the wall. Quentin picked up the hem of his robe and ran as fast as he could to return it. The ball took a wicked bounce off the wall and headed for the sloping roof of a low-built shed. Brother Mark pulled up his robe and scrambled onto the roof to hit the ball again.

As he slid off, a blur of bony knees and sandals, Quentin made a spectacular leap over a barrel. He pulled back his arm and hit the ball as hard as he could, blasting it past Brother Mark's right ear.

"Alas! You have taken me again, Brother Quentin," Mark said between gasps for air.

"Let me try," William said, stepping into the courtyard.

Quentin raised his eyebrows and smiled. "Make way for Sir William, the noble warrior and fearless knight!" he said in a taunting voice. William playfully punched his younger brother in the arm. Quentin looked at Flattop. "Would you care to challenge your friend?"

"Sure," Flattop answered. He played handball all the time at school. Except for jumping on sheds and over barrels, this was the same game.

Flattop picked up the ball and inspected it—pieces of leather tied with some kind of string. It looked a little like a baseball, but it was lighter and softer. He gave the ball a test bounce on the ground. It didn't have the springy-ness of the tennis balls he played with at school, so he knew he'd have to adjust his game.

He tossed the ball in the air and gave it a good hard smack. William ran forward and hit it. Flattop backed up, stepped over a barrel and hit the leather ball again, driving William to the back of the courtyard to return it. Then, Flattop lofted the ball high into the air. It lightly tapped the upper right corner of the wall and fell about two feet in front. William stumbled forward, but it was no use. He'd fallen for the old *sucker lob*.

Quentin walked over to Flattop and shook his hand. "Excellent strategy, my friend."

Flattop nodded. "Yeah, well, I play this at home."

Quentin smiled. "I imagine you do. 'Twas a French

knight who first brought the game to us. He said he learned it in the Holy Land during the Crusade."

Flattop wasn't eager to talk about France and he didn't have a clue what to say about handball and the Holy Land, so he just said, "I learned it at school a long time ago."

Quentin gasped, then looked at his brother. "William, you did not tell me Flattop was a scholar."

"I did not know he was," William said as he practiced lobbing the ball into the wall.

Flattop doubted whether Mrs. Penn or Ms. McVey would agree that he was a scholar, but he nodded anyway.

"I am a scribe," Quentin said. He took Flattop by the elbow and escorted him across the courtyard. "Come. You must visit our scriptorium." They walked to the doorway of a large room with rows of angled tabletops, the kind architects and engineers use.

A monk sat at each table with a book at his side. They studied the lines in their books, then carefully copied the words onto large pages of cream-colored paper.

Quentin spoke softly, "Here is where we transcribe our books. I have the honor of working on John of Salisbury's grammar book. As you know, he is a master on the subject."

"Yeah. Good ol' John," Flattop said, trying to sound smart. "I especially like the *e-d* rule."

Quentin tilted his head and looked confused.

"You know," Flattop explained, "adding an *e-d* when a verb is past tense."

"Ah . . . I see," Quentin said, but Flattop could tell he didn't.

"So this is where you write the books, huh?" Flattop hoped to get the conversation back on track.

"Oh, no. We merely copy them. The world awaits

as many volumes of Salisbury's grammar book as we can provide.''

Flattop tried to imagine what it would be like to copy a whole book. It made his hand ache just thinking about it. One of the monks was carefully placing a finished page on a table next to him. Flattop strained on his tiptoes to see what it looked like. ''Can we go in there?'' Flattop asked.

''Yes, but you must not speak. The brothers need silence so they may complete their task with no errors. We believe so strongly in this that we use sign language to communicate.'' Quentin led the way with Flattop following. They stopped at a table to watch an older monk carefully printing letters onto a page about twice the size of the paper Flattop used at school.

Flattop watched the monk's steady hand carefully draw each letter in black ink. He recognized the fancy squiggles and curlicues on the page—he always called it ''Shakespeare writing.'' His parents once dragged him to a junk store that used lettering like that in their sign: Ye Olde Antique Shoppe.

Flattop stepped a little closer to look over the monk's shoulder as he filled in another line of printing. The monk turned and smiled at Flattop and Quentin. He was probably as old as Flattop's grandfather, and had a round face and a friendly smile. Quentin began gesturing in sign language. The monk nodded and gestured back.

They both looked at Flattop.

Flattop waved.

Quentin escorted Flattop through the door on the other side of the room.

''That was Brother Edward. I introduced you.''

''Oh.'' Flattop looked back through the door. Maybe he should wave some more. He raised his hand, but

Brother Edward was already huddled over his work again. "I think he's really busy right now," Flattop said.

"We spend every hour of daylight on transcription. Luckily, we can work even longer with the approach of summer." Quentin walked to a wooden barrel and used a stick to stir the contents.

Flattop peeked over the rim. The smell reminded him of the time a dead seal washed up on the beach and no one found it for days. "What's that?"

" 'Tis the start of our book pages. When we make vellum, we soak calfskin in lime water. For parchment, we use sheepskin. The lime water allows us to remove the hair from the animal's hide."

Flattop nodded in agreement. "Yeah. You wouldn't want hairy paper."

Quentin led Flattop to an area in the sun where young boys scraped the hair off sheepskins, then stretched the skins and nailed them to something that looked like a wooden picture frame. They walked past rows of stretched skins left to dry in the sun. Quentin knelt to rub his finger on one, then picked up the frame and took it to an empty table.

Reaching for a stone that looked more like a sponge, Quentin said, "This is pumice. We rub the dried skin gently until it is thin and smooth. Then we cut the skin to the size of our books." He handed the pumice to Flattop. "Try it."

Flattop took the stone in his hand and leaned over the framed skin.

"Gently," Quentin reminded him.

Flattop began to lightly rub the stone across the skin. Dried-up shreds of gunk pulled loose with each stroke. He looked up at Quentin and smiled.

"The task is to make the skin the same thickness on the sides as it is in the center."

Flattop twisted the stone in his hand to fit it more snugly against the wooden frame. He pulled down slowly, watching chunks and strands release and roll up in front of the pumice. "This is cool!" Flattop said. "Has William seen this?"

Quentin shook his head. "My brother has no interest in books."

Flattop pulled the pumice away from the dried skin. "Didn't he have books in school?"

"William chose to be a knight, in hopes that his service to a nobleman would earn him a parcel of land."

"So . . . William didn't go to school?"

"It is far more important for my brother to know how to defend himself than it is to know how to read."

Flattop's eyes practically popped out of his head. "William doesn't know how to read?"

"Why, no. Neither does James." Quentin reached for the pumice stone in Flattop's hand and placed it next to the frame. "Reading is woman's work. My mother read. She taught the girls in our castle to read."

"But you said that you—"

"With both of my brothers becoming knights, there was no place to foster me for battle training. My father had donated much to the monastery, so they took me in. Reading, studying, and transcribing books are at the center of our lives here."

Flattop wanted to say he felt sorry for Quentin, since he didn't have a choice in what he wanted to be. But knowing that William—who could shoot a bow and arrow, hunt with a hawk, and tell dramatic stories at inns—couldn't read a first-grade book made him feel more sorry for William.

The bell above the chapel rang.

Quentin looked in the direction of the sound. "Flattop, you must forgive me. It is time for Terce and Mass."

"Huh?"

"We attend chapel seven times a day," Quentin said. "It is time for our third prayer service, and I regret that I must leave you now."

Flattop's mom and dad always warned him not to overstay his welcome. Now he felt he had. "Hey, that's okay," Flattop said, feeling his cheeks flush with embarrassment. "William and I have to hit the road anyway."

Quentin and Flattop walked back through the scriptorium, where the monks were leaving their work and heading to the chapel. They entered the cloisters, where William stood alone, still hitting the handball against the wall.

"My brother," Quentin said, his arms outstretched. "I must leave you now and take my place in the chapel. If you should wish to stay the night, I might be able to arrange it with the abbot."

"No thank you, Quentin." William looked down at the leather-covered ball in his hand. "Lord Wickshire awaits my arrival." He handed the ball to Quentin. "Take care of yourself, my brother."

"Godspeed, William."

Flattop watched the two brothers say good-bye. He wondered when they'd see each other again. They hugged tightly then slapped each other on the back. For the first time since he'd returned to the Middle Ages, he missed his mom and dad. And even Marcia.

The chapel bell continued to ring. "Come, Flattop," William said. "Let us tarry no longer."

"Yes. You must not keep James waiting," Quentin said. He looked at the monks filing into the chapel, then pointed to the back of the courtyard. "You may pass through the scriptorium to reach the stables and retrieve your mounts."

"Aye." William nodded and turned around. "Come, Flattop."

Flattop followed him across the courtyard, although he was beginning to feel a little like a dog, the way William was always saying, "Come, Flattop."

"Give Alice my best wishes," Quentin called out to them.

"Aye," William said, though he didn't stop walking or even glance back at Quentin.

Flattop looked over his shoulder at Quentin and waved. "We will . . . and thanks . . . for the tour and everything."

Quentin nodded, then hurried to the chapel.

William and Flattop got their horses out of the stable, then trotted through the monastery gate and up a rocky hill toward Wickshire. When they reached the top, William stopped a minute to look back. Flattop pulled up beside him and looked out over the green valley where the convent and monastery sat side by side. The fields were empty now. The monks were in prayer. Flattop thought he saw a sad look in William's eyes.

"It's too bad we have to leave so soon, huh?" Flattop said, trying to console him.

"Aye . . . " William paused, then took a deep breath and pushed his shoulders back. "We have wasted too much time here. Let us be on our way," William said, then slapped his horse's reins and trotted down the other side of the hill, never looking back.

9

Flattop pushed up the sleeve of his jacket to check his watch. Noon. He shifted his weight in the saddle for the millionth time. The last hour had been a quiet one.

He glanced at William, a good fifty yards ahead of him now. Every time Flattop tried to catch up, William rode faster. Flattop remembered when his best friend, Jason, lost his dog. He didn't want to talk to anyone, either.

Flattop's stomach grumbled. It had been hours since they'd eaten those sausages at Blanche's inn. "Hey, William," he shouted. "How much longer before we get to Wickshire castle? I'm starving."

William didn't answer. Instead, he guided his horse under the shade of a tree and dismounted. By the time Flattop reached him, he was sitting on the grass, opening a linen cloth to reveal some dried meat. He tore off a chunk and offered the rest to Flattop. "Venison," he said. "From Lady Hemstead's cookhouse."

Flattop bit off a few salty, leathery strings and held them in his mouth until he worked up enough spit to chew. "How long has it been since you've seen Quentin?"

William leaned back against the tree trunk. He sighed, looked out over the countryside, then took a bite of venison and chewed slowly. "Quentin was fostered to the Benedictine monastery when he had seen seven winters. I was a page at Hemstead castle by then. However, we both returned to my father's lands to attend the tournament held when my brother, James, was dubbed a knight."

"They let Quentin out of the monastery for a tournament?"

William laughed. "The monastery is not a prison, my friend."

"Then how come you two don't see each other more?"

"He has his work and I have mine. Also, as a Benedictine brother, he has given up owning property. He has no horse or cart of his own to use for travel. When James was dubbed, my father had to send a wagon for him."

Flattop finally swallowed the dried venison. "Did your father send a wagon for you, too?"

"I attended because I was the squire in service to Sir Humphrey. He was invited to compete in James's first tournament. I accompanied him to Wickshire."

Flattop bent a pointed corner of the dried venison back and forth until it broke off in his hand. If William and Quentin had cars, it wouldn't be such a big deal to see each other. They could just hop in, turn the key, and drive. He looked at the tall grass and clumps of rocks. A Jeep would be even better.

"I saw Quentin again after the blight of smallpox took its toll on Wickshire Castle." William picked a few random blades of grass. "We helped James bury our parents, our other brother, and our only sister. That was in my twelfth winter."

Twelve years old? Sorrow stabbed Flattop in the chest

as he tried to imagine losing his mom and dad at the age he was right now. "I'm sorry, William," he said. "I don't know what I'd do if I didn't have my mom and dad around."

William looked up at him, then narrowed his gaze. "Flattop, your parents are dead, remember? You said they were killed by the Robber King."

Flattop felt his mouth drop open and a tiny gasp escape. *Stupid, stupid, stupid!* He hated lying. He wasn't any good at it. And now he was caught.

"You are an orphan, are you not?" William prompted.

Flattop started to sweat. "Uh . . . yeah. I'm an orphan." He repeated his old story, hoping to get a running start into a new lie. "I was traveling with my parents—and the Robber King killed us. Them! I mean, them! Then—you know—I helped you kill the Robber King."

William studied Flattop closely. "Aye. If you say it is so."

Flattop began to squirm. "I guess it's still too new to me. The dying and everything." He crossed his fingers on both hands so the dead-parents lie wouldn't jinx him. When William didn't say anything else, Flattop cleared his throat, then got up. He dusted off his baseball uniform, checking the seat of his pants for grass stains. "Well, we'd better get going, huh?" He walked to his horse.

William stayed seated. "Flattop, where are you from?"

Flattop wheeled around. "I told you. France."

"But my brother has never heard of the California region of France." William slowly rose to his feet. "And my brother is very learned."

Flattop pulled off his baseball cap, rubbed his fingers through his hair, then put his cap back on, adjusting and readjusting it. "I know. It—it's a new section. It's not on the maps yet." He shoved a foot in one stirrup and hiked himself onto the saddle. "Come on, William. We're gonna be late."

William reached for Flattop's reins. "You say you are a noble, yet you do not dress like one. You are not skilled in arms or horsemanship. You know of books, yet you do not wear the clothes of a scholar or a monk. Who are you, Flattop Kincaid?"

For half a second, Flattop almost told him the truth—the Red Sox, the Wizard, his computer, dark glass and all. But he remembered the Wizard's warning the first time he traveled through history: *"Watch that you do not dazzle them with knowledge from your century, unless you want to be tortured for practicing witchcraft."*

"Who am I?" Flattop repeated, giving himself a little more time. "You want to know who I am?" All that stalling and he still hadn't come up with anything better than what he'd already told William. "I'm Flattop Kincaid from California. It's a new place. It isn't on your brother's maps yet. I don't have any family or friends here. I'm all alone."

In the silence that followed, Flattop had time to digest what he'd said. *I'm all alone.* That was truer than he wanted to admit. He hadn't seen Alice since she left Hemstead, and he hadn't talked to the Wizard since he'd left his century to live the good life and hang around with Alison Wedertz's ancestors. Maybe it'd been a stupid idea to come back here.

William handed Flattop the reins. "Very well," he said. "I believe you." He climbed on his horse and galloped out about fifty yards ahead of Flattop before motioning for him to follow.

The afternoon ride through the muddy grass was better than Flattop expected. At one point, when the horses had to wade through a stream, William even waited up for Flattop so they could cross it together. William talked about thieves and highwaymen who were the curse of civilized man, with their low morals and disregard for human life and property. Flattop substituted bank robbers and carjackers for William's words and realized some things hadn't changed much in hundreds of years.

The setting sun was beginning to touch the tops of the trees behind them when William paused. In the distance, perched on the highest hill around, stood Wickshire Castle. Flattop didn't have to ask—it looked exactly like the picture Alison Wedertz had shown him. Except her castle was falling apart and had tour buses and an ice cream truck parked in front of it.

"Look, Flattop," William said, a catch in his voice. " 'Tis my home."

Flattop couldn't wait to see another reunion of William and one of his brothers. "What're we waiting for? Let's go!"

Before Flattop could kick his heels into his horse's sides, William was already galloping down the hill as fast as his horse could carry him.

"Hey!" Flattop shouted. "Wait up!"

William didn't slow down until he reached the drawbridge. "I am Sir William of Wickshire," he announced loudly enough for people to hear him ten miles away. "I have come to take my place beside my brother, Lord Wickshire."

"William!" An old woman shouted. She gathered her

long, beige tunic and hurried down the drawbridge toward him. "Welcome home, lad!" She looked up at him, her eyes filled with the kind of pride Flattop's mom and dad got when there weren't any *D*'s or *F*'s on his report card.

William sat a little straighter in his saddle. "Good nurse, I have been dubbed a knight while in the service of Lord Hemstead. I will thank you to call me *Sir,* not *lad.*"

Flattop sighed. It looked like the old, stuck-up William was back.

"*Sir,* indeed!" The woman laughed, showing several spaces where teeth should be. Then she slapped William on the thigh. "I held you to my breast, boy. Do not take that high-and-mighty tone with me."

Instead of getting mad like Flattop thought he would, William laughed and reached for her hand. "Forgive me, good nurse. You are as fair and lovely as the day I left. I remain your humble servant." He bent down and kissed her hand.

The woman's face blushed scarlet and she giggled like a little girl. She pinched William's cheek and said softly, "That is more like it, lad. Now stable your horse and I shall tell Lord Wickshire of your arrival."

"Aye, nurse," William said.

The woman scurried through the big gate, across the alley and onto the inner drawbridge, calling, "William has arrived! Our William is home!"

William and Flattop rode their horses up the drawbridge and through the gate.

Flattop asked, "That was your nurse?"

"Aye, she raised me."

"You must've been sick a lot," Flattop concluded.

"No, I warrant you, I was full of good health."

"Then why did you need a nurse?" Flattop asked.

William smiled. "She nursed me when I was a baby."

Flattop gasped. "You mean, that stuff about holding you to her—her—"

"Aye." William stopped and looked at Flattop. "Did you not have a woman to care for you and nurse you when you were a baby?"

Flattop felt the corners of his mouth turn down in disgust. "Yeah, but she was my *mom*. Using another lady is kind of . . . sick."

William shook his head and shrugged. "I fear we have found another way in which your California customs differ from ours." With that, William nudged his heels into his horses's ribs and turned left down the narrow cobblestone alley. Flattop followed, watching chicken and geese flutter out of the way.

With every clip-clop of their horses' hooves, more people poured into the alley to welcome Sir William home. The workers in the cookhouse and bakery ran out, wiping the sweat off their foreheads with the sleeves of their tunics. Flattop glanced over his shoulder to see a crowd of cheering people following them.

As William led him past the brewery, Flattop realized the open stalls of the workers were located in the same areas as the stalls in Hemstead castle. He was glad to know he wouldn't get lost.

A young girl with a basket of flowers handed a daisy to William. He thanked her and tucked it into his horses's mane. As they turned the corner, Flattop saw a familiar sign ahead. The Mews. The Hawk House. He wondered if the Wizard might hide in a little hawk like he'd often done at Hemstead castle.

He reached in his back pocket to make sure the

dark glass was still there, and smiled when his fingers slid across its smooth, cool surface.

The blacksmith put down his hammer and left his fires to lean against the doorway, his smile flashing even brighter against his soot-blackened face. The carpenter laid down the chunk of wood he was carving and joined the crowd.

William and Flattop passed the pigpens where buckets of garbage were being thrown into troughs, and the cow stalls where stable workers raked through the hay and mud. When they finally arrived at the livery and dismounted, Flattop noticed they had traveled the complete circle of the alley. Leave it to William to make a big deal out of riding in so everybody would see him.

After handing their reins to stable boys, William and Flattop walked up to the inner drawbridge. On the other side, a tall, muscular man with coal-black hair took a wide stance and placed his hands on his hips. Flattop thought he looked a lot like Superman, except he had a mustache and a little beard that just covered his chin. And instead of a big red S on his chest, he wore a yellow tunic with a royal blue dragon on the front.

William knelt on one knee. '' 'Tis I, Lord Wickshire.''

Flattop's brow furrowed. This was James? Where was the big, brotherly reunion like he'd seen with Quentin and William? Where was the headlock? The good-natured punch in the stomach?

''You may approach,'' Lord Wickshire's booming voice echoed off the high stone walls.

William rose to his feet and walked stiffly across the bridge, with Flattop following close behind. William stopped in front of his brother and, without warning, knelt on one knee again, leaving Flattop exposed to Lord Wickshire's fiercely intense glare.

"Sorry," Flattop mumbled and stepped to the side.

William raised both hands to Lord Wickshire, who clasped them firmly.

"Sir William," James said, "do you wish to be my man?"

"I wish it," William answered.

Flattop frowned. This was getting a little weird.

William cleared his throat and announced, "I promise by my faith that, from this time forward, I will be loyal to Lord Wickshire and will maintain toward him my homage entirely against every man, in good faith and without deception."

Lord Wickshire commanded, "Rise, Sir William." William stood up and the two brothers kissed each other on the cheek. Flattop would rather have seen a headlock.

Lord Wickshire stood back while everyone cheered and hugged William. "Welcome home," he said.

10

"Philip!" Lord Wickshire commanded. "Show them to their chamber!"

A boy who was about Flattop's age nodded and ran up the donjon stairs.

"My lord," William said, as he signaled for Flattop to step forward. "This is the brave noble from California who helped me dispatch the Robber King and his band of thieves."

Lord Wickshire stood perfectly still, staring at Flattop—making him very nervous.

Flattop started to bite his lip, then asked, "Do you want me to do that kneeling thing William just did?"

Lord Wickshire scowled for another second, then he roared with laughter and slapped Flattop on the back. " 'Kneeling thing'!" He laughed some more. "Off with you!"

"As you wish, Lord Wickshire," William said, bowing slightly. He and Flattop walked to the top of the stairs where Philip waited.

"Hey, William," Flattop half-whispered. "What was all that 'be my man' stuff about?"

"You mean, my oath to James?" William glanced over his shoulder as he pulled open the thick, wooden door at the top of the stairs. "In order for me to live here and share the bounty my brother provides, I must swear to be loyal and defend him in all matters."

"How come I didn't have to do that?" Flattop asked.

"You are a guest here for as long as my brother wishes to extend his hospitality. Your loyalty is not demanded." William turned. "But it *is* expected."

The Great Hall looked like the one at Hemstead castle. Torches burned in their iron holders on the walls, tables and benches were arranged in rows, and there was a platform with a long table where all the important people ate.

Back in Flattop's century, a lot of the houses in his neighborhood looked alike. That meant he always knew where the kitchen was, and he didn't have to ask for directions to the backyard. Apparently, castles were designed the same way, too.

Philip led William and Flattop across the room to the stone stairs leading up to the next level. He took two thick candles and held the wicks up to a wall torch, then gave one to William. They walked up the steps and past a row of doors to a narrower set of stairs at the other end.

"Hey, William. Didn't we just pass the bedrooms?"

"Those are the bedchambers for honored guests— visiting lords and ladies," William said. "Here, in Wickshire, I am a member of the family. My chamber is close to my brother's, at the very top of the donjon."

Philip led them up more stairs. Flattop grimaced. His calves were beginning to cramp from all the stair climbing. When they reached the top, he grabbed one of the rough-cut blocks of stone in the wall to steady himself, then lowered his heels over the edge of the last step to stretch his calf muscles.

There were dark hallways leading to the left and right. Straight ahead were two big wooden doors with black iron hinges. William nodded toward them. "That is the Great Chamber, where Lord and Lady Wickshire reside."

"You mean Alice lives in there?"

William nodded. "And James."

Flattop thought about Alice being pregnant and having to climb all those stairs. "It seems kind of dumb for the most important people in the castle to be so far up here."

"It is for their protection," William said. "If the castle were to come under siege, the family can hide here. An attacker would have to fight every man in the castle before he could get this far."

"If you please, Sir William." Philip motioned for him to enter the hall that led to the left.

As they walked through the corridor, Flattop looked over his shoulder. "What's down the other way?"

"Ladies' bedchambers," William answered. "When my mother and father lived in the Great Chamber, my sister had a room on that side. My brothers and I were over here. James's children will one day occupy these rooms."

"What'll happen to you?"

William shrugged. "I shall take a chamber on the lower floor, or I will sleep on a table in the Great Hall."

Serfs like John and Ruth slept on their dinner tables all the time. But here was William, a knight, who might have to do the same thing. Flattop shook his head. William might be a little conceited, but he didn't deserve to be treated like a peasant, especially when his brother owned the whole castle.

Philip stopped in front of one of the closed doors.

William thanked him and patted him on the shoulder. "Tell Lord Wickshire we are most grateful for his kindness." Flattop stepped aside as Philip ran past.

Flattop squinted to see what lay further ahead in the dark corridor. "Are there more stairs?"

"Aye," William said. "They lead to the gallery."

The only gallery Flattop knew about was an art gallery. "You mean, you've got paintings and stuff up there?"

"No." William chuckled. " 'Tis where the archers are stationed if the castle is under attack."

"Cool! Can I see it?"

"Aye. Come with me." William held the candle up to light the way. The hall got narrower with every step. Flattop remembered a fun house at the county fair where the walkway got smaller and smaller until you practically had to crawl on your hands and knees.

William reached the other end of the corridor and pushed the door open. Daylight spilled in, blinding Flattop. William put his candle in the wall holder and walked out on the roof. Flattop followed, blinking.

"The gallery," William said.

Flattop looked at the slotted pattern of the gray stone blocks. It looked just like the castle towers in the movies. He walked to the edge and crouched behind a set of higher blocks. "This is where the archers hide, huh?" he said, raising an imaginary bow and arrow. He leaned out over the lower blocks, pretended to shoot, then took aim again.

" 'Tis a strong defense," William replied. "We not only have a clear shot, we can also see what the enemy will do next."

Flattop stood up and looked over the edge. The height

reminded him of the time he had to go with his mom to the tenth floor of an office building in Los Angeles.

Flattop walked around the perimeter of the gallery, looking at the drawbridges and the circular cobblestone walkways below. "Hey!" He motioned for William to join him. "There's the alley we rode through."

"You mean the *bailey?*"

"The what?" Flattop glanced at William.

"The bailey. 'Tis a pathway for wagons and horses within the castle walls."

Flattop peered over the edge of the gallery again. "In California, we call them alleys."

William pointed toward the outer drawbridge. "The outer bailey is used by the serfs and craftsmen. Anyone who comes across the outer drawbridge will use the outer bailey." He put a hand on Flattop's shoulder. "However, if you are a guest of Wickshire, a visiting noble, or a servant in the donjon, you are allowed to cross the inner drawbridge and use the inner bailey."

Flattop looked into the courtyard below with its flowers, trees, and benches, and he thought of seven-year-old Margaret. Now that she was a chambermaid, she'd get to walk around the inner bailey at Hemstead castle and see how pretty the courtyard was. Then she could tell the rest of her family what it looked like.

"Come. We must prepare to attend Lord Wickshire." William pulled the door open, took the burning candle out of the holder, and walked down the corridor to their bedchamber with Flattop following close behind.

William pushed open the chamber door, walked inside, and raised the candle higher. The flame created spooky shadows on the gray stone walls. Flattop paused at the threshold and studied the room.

Two wooden boxes that looked like toy chests stood

at the far wall. A great big, blue-and-brown rug hung above them. The bed was wider than the one at Hemstead, but it had the same kind of wooden posts that rose up out of the four corners and supported a dark wood frame overhead.

"This is the bedchamber I shared with my brothers," William said.

"You mean you and Quentin and James all slept in that bed?" Suddenly the bed didn't look that big.

"And Andrew—the brother we lost."

"*Four* of you in that little bed?" Now it looked tiny.

William chuckled. "James was fostered out the year I was born. So Andrew, Quentin, and I shared it. By the time James returned home, Andrew and I were fostered out. It was never really crowded."

Flattop sat on the mattress. Puffy. He pulled back the covers and smelled that chicken coop odor. Another down mattress. He wasn't complaining, down mattresses were more comfortable than straw. He just wished they smelled better.

He looked overhead and saw dark blue fabric covering the frame. "Hey look, William," Flattop said as he stood at the edge of the bed. "This navy blue . . . that's the color Blanche was wearing at the inn, remember?"

" 'Tis indigo, not blue," William said. "From the indigo plant. Dyers must use a very special process to make the color this dark and rich."

Flattop tugged on the rolled edge of the fabric and it toppled down, draping the entire side of the bed. "Curtains!" Flattop laughed. "You could make a really cool fort out of a bed like this." When he saw William's puzzled look, he walked around the frame, tugging the

70

rest of the indigo fabric until it fell down around the bed. "Here. I'll show you."

William followed behind him, rolling the cloth back into place. "This prevents the night air from bringing diseases while you sleep."

"Huh?" Flattop turned and looked at William, sure he was kidding. The solemn look on William's face told him otherwise.

"Fresh air, especially night air, is very bad for your health." He gave the indigo material an extra push onto the wooden frame. "Sleeping with this pulled down reduces illness and death."

Flattop thought about that for a minute, then broke out in a fit of laughter. "Death? From night air? I don't think so!"

William glared at him. "It has been proven by many learned scientists," he said coldly.

Proven? By scientists? Flattop stopped laughing. Maybe this was like the poison-apple thing. Apples might be poison in the Middle Ages, but not in Flattop's century. Maybe night air *wasn't* safe in 1150 A.D. He cleared his throat, a little ashamed. "I'm sorry. I just never heard that before."

"It is possible that your California has not caught up with the many scientific achievements of my country."

Before Flattop could disagree, there was a knock on the door.

"Enter," William said.

The door opened and Alice walked in and curtsied.

"Alice!" Flattop ran over to her. "How are you? Are you ready to have your baby?"

Alice laughed then rested her hand on the piles of black and white fabric gathered over her stomach. "Not yet, lad."

William stood at attention beside the bed. "Does my brother wish to see me?" he asked.

"No," Alice said. "I have come to prepare your bath."

With that, a parade of women and children entered, carrying buckets and pitchers of water. They walked through the bedchamber to the small adjoining room and poured them into a big wooden tub.

Alice turned to William. "I trust your journey was easy."

"Aye," William said, as he unbelted his sword and laid it on the bed.

"We stayed at an inn and ate sausage," Flattop volunteered.

"Hart's Blood Inn," William added as he tugged the white tunic over his head and laid it next to his sword.

"Blanche says hello," Flattop remembered to tell her.

"Thank you, Flattop. I know her well. She is a good and honest businesswoman."

William lifted the hooded, chain mail tunic over his head and placed it on the bed.

As the last servant left the room, Alice curtsied to William. "I shall leave you to your bath, Sir William. Flattop, I shall see you at supper."

"Hey, wait! You want me to help you with something? I could—" The door closed before Flattop could finish. He turned to William. "Did you see how funny she was acting?"

William sat on the bed and took off his boots.

"William?" Flattop didn't like being ignored.

"Hmmm?"

"Alice was acting weird."

William headed for the bathtub. "I noticed nothing unusual."

"She was curtseying all over the place and calling you sir. You never noticed?"

William stopped and turned to face Flattop. "Of course she was. I am a knight. And I shall thank you to show the same respect when we are in the company of others."

"Huh?"

"I am called *Sir* William now. When we are alone, you may call me William. But when others are present, you must call me Sir out of respect for my station in life." He walked through the bathing-room door.

Flattop stood in the bedchamber trying to figure out what was wrong with his friend. He decided to make one more try. "You're kidding, right?"

William ducked back into the room. "I am most serious. And Flattop," he warned, "she is *Lady Wickshire,* not Alice." Then he disappeared into the bathing room.

A mixture of anger and embarrassment turned Flattop's ears so hot, he thought they might burst into flames. He remembered when one of Marcia's friends got to be a cheerleader and stopped hanging out with her. His sister cried for days over that. At the time he thought Marcia was being stupid.

Now he knew how it felt.

11

Flattop went down to the Great Hall for supper. He was alone. Not because he wanted to be, but because William didn't wait for him. He told Flattop that other knights and their squires would be arriving tonight for tomorrow's feast and the tournament the next day. He needed to stand beside his brother in the Great Hall and welcome them.

Who stood beside James before you got here? That's what Flattop wanted to say. But instead, he told William to go ahead.

Flattop took his turn in the dirty, lukewarm bath water, then got dressed. He didn't have much energy for Coach Hartman's dressing ceremony, though. Instead he thought about William's dressing ceremony to be a knight. White tunic meant knights were supposed to be pure and obey God's law.

"But I guess it's okay to stomp all over your friends and act like you're a big deal," Flattop muttered as he pulled his uniform pants over his socks.

William's red robe meant he should be ready to pour out his blood for the Holy Church. "I'd like to pour out some of his blood," Flattop grumbled. He thought about William's first tournament, the day after tomorrow. Maybe one of the knights *Sir* William wanted to hang around with would pour out some of William's blood. That'd teach him a lesson about who his real friends were.

Flattop put on his cleats and double-knotted the laces. He tugged his T-shirt with the long red sleeves over his head, and pulled on his V-necked jersey with the red satin letters that spelled RED SOX across the chest. He ran his hand across the letters. "A Red Sox player has miles and miles and miles of heart." Miles and miles and miles of empty heart.

When Flattop finally arrived at the Great Hall, he saw six guys wearing different-colored tunics all talking to James. "Knights," Flattop muttered. "Big deal."

There was a lot of hand shaking—actually, they just clasped hands. William was standing at attention next to James, and it looked like he was being introduced. The rest of the knights were slapping each other on the back and laughing, but William didn't look all that comfortable.

Flattop walked around the room, looking at banners hanging from the ceiling and pushing the toe of his cleat through the rushes on the floor.

"Flattop?" a familiar female voice said.

He turned to find Alice standing behind him, her green eyes warm and bright.

"Hi, Ali—" Flattop remembered the lecture William had given him earlier. If anyone in this whole stupid castle deserved respect, it was Alice. He looked down, ashamed he hadn't treated her better. "I mean, *Lady Wickshire.*"

Alice pulled away from him slightly. "My goodness. What has come over you?"

"William says I don't respect you when I call you

Alice. He says I have to call you Lady Wickshire." He shrugged, then glanced at William. "And I have to call *him* Sir William."

"I see," Alice said, nodding her head. "I was right. It has already happened."

"What has?"

"I am afraid your friend has gotten rather full of himself," Alice said. "It usually comes with being dubbed a knight."

Flattop felt a grin take over his old frown. "It does?"

"Oh, yes," Alice said, pretending to be very serious. "Warriors are often an insufferable breed."

Flattop looked up at her. "Insufferable, huh?"

" 'Tis their duty in life to tell great tales of their adventures. 'Tis *our* duty to look properly impressed." Her green eyes sparkled.

"Yeah, well, William hasn't really had any adventures yet—except killing the Robber King, and he's already exaggerating that." Flattop looked over at William, who was once again acting out his struggle with the Robber King for the other knights. William's new, improved version of the story had him shouting, punching, and wrestling with the villain instead of shooting one arrow through the man's heart.

Alice chuckled. "A knight is expected to add bold splashes of color to his stories. 'Tis part of his charm, his power. Our knights also write beautiful poetry and compose songs for the women they love."

Flattop looked back at her. "They can't even read."

"No, but they can speak—and as you can see by your friend's story, they speak well."

"Does James write you poetry?" Flattop asked.

Alice smoothed the gathered material of her black-

and-white dress. "Goodness, no. I have been his wife much too long for that."

"Did he used to?"

Alice's cheeks turned pink. "No. But courtly love is very different than marriage. Courtly love addresses a woman's ability to inspire a man to greatness. Marriage is a legal and binding contract." She glanced toward James, then smiled. "Our marriage was arranged by our fathers to join our land holdings."

Flattop had heard that people in the olden days got married for business reasons, but he'd never actually met anyone who had. "So . . . you and James don't love each other?"

"Of course we do," she answered. "But it is a love borne out of duty to each other and to our lands."

Flattop couldn't imagine anyone not loving Alice for the nice person she was, land or no land.

Alice nodded toward the group of knights. "I think Sir William has finished his story."

Flattop looked at the group. "It takes him longer to tell it than it did to happen."

Alice laughed softly. "Once William has a few more victories to his name, his stories will be easier to abide. Perhaps the tournament will yield him a conquest or two, then he can talk about that."

"Is James in the tournament?"

Flattop figured he was big enough and mean enough to win it all.

Alice shook her head. "No. He is the host. Besides, he is far too important to risk injury or death in a contest."

Flattop gasped. "You mean—William could get killed?"

"Aye." Alice nodded. "It has happened before. These are war games. And our warriors are in earnest."

Flattop remembered back in the bedchamber when he wished for William's blood to pour out. Now he wished he hadn't wished for that. He stared at the laces on his shoes and concentrated with all his might. *I take it back, I take it back, I take it back.*

"Woman!"

Flattop looked up to see who was calling.

"Woman!" James shouted again.

Alice half-whispered to Flattop, "I must leave you. My husband calls." She scurried over to James and curtsied. "I beg your pardon, my lord. I was just this moment conversing with William's noble friend from Calif—"

"Sweet Mary, woman!" James interrupted.

Alice curtsied again. "What is it you require of me, my lord?"

"I shall require that you hold your tongue!" James said, laughing.

"Yes, my lord," she said, then blushed bright red as William and all the knights roared with laughter.

Flattop scowled. Funny how William wanted Flattop to treat Alice with respect, then he stood in a group of guys and laughed while her husband made fun of her.

12

Flattop stormed down the donjon steps to the inner bailey. He stopped and took a deep breath, glad to be away from William, James, and all the knights who'd laughed at Alice.

A twinge of guilt gnawed at his insides. He should've done something to defend her. "Quit picking on her!" he should've said. But he probably would've ended up dead, with a bunch of knights' swords stuck in him. He tightened his fists and pounded them into his thighs. Why did knights have to be such bullies? And why did he have to be such a coward?

When he got upset like this at a Little League game, Coach Hartman always told him to walk it off.

So he did.

He walked across the inner drawbridge to the outer bailey. It was getting dark and most of the workers were hurrying to close up. The baker had already gone. The carpenter and the blacksmith, too. Flattop turned toward the wall, pulled up his sleeve, and checked his watch. Almost six o'clock.

He needed to talk to the Wizard. Pulling the dark glass from his back pocket, he searched the sky. If he could capture the moon's reflection in the glass, the

Wizard would appear. But the moon wasn't out. He walked to the Mews. Maybe the Wizard had found a hawk to hide in.

When Flattop pushed open the creaky wooden door, he heard a flutter of wings, then silence. Slowly he scanned the room. Seeing no people inside, he tiptoed into the shadows and found four birds perched in their cages.

"Wizard?" he whispered. "Are you in here?"

Nothing.

"Wizard, I need to talk to you."

One of the hawks ruffled its feathers.

Flattop's heart filled with hope. He stood in front of the hawk's cage, straining to see the bird through the darkening shadows. "Is that you, Wizard?" he asked.

The bird didn't move.

All Flattop wanted to do was look in its eyes. "Come here, birdie," he said, then puckered his lips and made kissing sounds. "Here, birdie, birdie." He smiled to show the hawk he was friendly.

Finally, the hawk crept into the light. Flattop took off his hat and pushed his head close to the cage bars. He tried to focus on the slitted pupils of the hawk's eyes. It just looked like a bird to him. He pressed his face tighter against the cage . . . looking . . . hoping—

The hawk screeched and lunged at his face.

"Augh!" Flattop screamed, falling backward.

The hawk fluttered back into the shadows.

"Stupid bird!" Flattop scolded as he got up and dusted himself off. "Stupid, dumb bird!" He stormed out of the Mews and into the alley, shoving his cap back on his head. "Stupid Wizard," he muttered bitterly.

Walk it off. He heard Coach Hartman's voice in the back of his mind. *Walk it off.*

80

Actually, he stomped it off, all the way around the outer bailey.

His mood didn't improve. How was he supposed to catch the Wizard if the guy wouldn't show up? Flattop was sick of the Middle Ages. He didn't care about Alison Wedertz's ancestors or living as a noble. He just wanted to find the Wizard and go home. He decided to take his mind off the agony of waiting by collecting a souvenir—something to take home as proof of where he'd been. Something better than a stupid apple.

Rocks, stones, dirt, and flowers wouldn't do, since no one would believe they came from Wickshire Castle. He needed something that said Wickshire Castle on it, like those spoons his grandmother collected from the Golden Gate Bridge and Disneyland. He'd have to keep his eyes open for the perfect thing.

By the time he reached the inner drawbridge for the second time, he was happy with his new plan of action and tired enough to go to bed, but the creak and clunk of a wagon pulling up behind him captured his attention, and he turned to watch.

A big, beefy man sat in the driver's seat, holding the reins in his chubby hands. He wore a heavy-looking cloak that had brown fur trim around the collar, and he had several gold rings on his fingers.

Then Flattop saw the girl. She sat beside the man, her hands folded in her lap. She was about Marcia's age, but a lot prettier. Of course, Marcia *was* his sister, so he probably couldn't judge. But one thing was for sure, this girl knew how to dress up. Her dark hair was pulled back into a fancy-looking gold hair net and a thin, shiny, gold band ran across her forehead. Where her cloak parted, Flattop could see the gleam of a red satin dress.

Whew! Flattop thought. *She must be rich!* He'd always been treated well in the Middle Ages because his jacket was made of red satin, but she had a whole dress of it. The man climbed down from the wagon, walked to the other side, and helped the girl down. She was so graceful, she practically floated to the ground.

"Welcome, Lord Faversham!" James's voice boomed. Flattop turned to see James, William, and Alice approaching from the donjon. "I am pleased you could come."

The man smiled and crossed the inner drawbridge, his hand outstretched. "Lord Wickshire! 'Tis an honor to be here! You remember my daughter, Rosalinde, do you not?"

"Aye," James said softly, then stepped forward to kneel before her. "Who could forget such a fair beauty?"

Rosalinde gently laughed, then gave a graceful curtsy. "Thank you, Lord Wickshire. You are as charming as ever."

Flattop scowled. He'd seen some first-class flirting between Marcia and just about every guy she met, but James was married—and his wife was standing right beside him.

Flattop watched James introduce William to Rosalinde. William acted like a bigger goof than his brother, bowing and kneeling and telling her she was pretty. When Rosalinde started to ask William how he liked being home, James interrupted and ordered Alice to show Lord Faversham and Rosalinde to their bedchambers.

Nodding obediently, Alice led the way up the donjon steps with Lord Faversham, Rosalinde, and James following. William stood motionless, staring after Rosalinde.

When everyone else had gone inside, Flattop started

for the stairs himself. He walked past William and said, "I'm going to bed."

William grabbed Flattop's arm. "Flattop! My friend! Did you not behold that beautiful creature?"

Friend? When had he become William's *friend* again? "Yeah, I saw her."

"*Saw* her?" William chuckled. "No. You did not merely *see* her. She is a vision. A feast for the eyes. A banquet of grace and loveliness, a—"

"Whatever," Flattop grumbled. "I'm going to bed."

"How can you think of sleep now that you have seen one of God's own angels?" William asked.

"It's easy. I'm tired. Goodnight." Flattop trudged up the stairs and opened the door.

"Should you want me for anything, I shall be here, composing a poem to her beauty."

"Uh-huh," Flattop said as he entered the Great Hall and pulled the door shut. He rolled his eyes, then went to his room to sleep away the rest of this weird night.

Flattop woke to the sound of William's poetry:

> *"Oh, fair and lovely Rosalinde,*
> *You have captured my very soul,*
> *Your breath is like the sweetest wind,*
> *And I—*
> *If I—"*

William stood in the middle of the bedchamber, squinting into the air. "What rhymes with *soul?*"

"Bowl?" Flattop muttered.

William snapped his fingers. "*Bowl!*" He frowned. "Hmmm. *Bowl.* No, that will not do."

"Troll?"

"Flattop, I do not believe you are truly trying to help me."

"What was your first clue?"

William pounded his head against one of the wooden bedposts, then sighed. "I fear you do not appreciate my dire situation."

"Your poetry stinks. So does mine." Flattop yawned and rubbed his eyes. "I never get better than a *C* on any poetry assignment, but it's no big deal."

William sat on the edge of the bed and rested his head in his hands. "Flattop, please. Tomorrow is my first tournament. I was hoping to win the favor of Rosalinde before I do battle."

You should be thinking about not getting killed, Flattop thought. But when he studied William's face, he was pretty sure he saw desperation in it. "Goal?"

"What?"

"*Goal* rhymes with *soul*."

William stood up, as if suddenly inspired. "I have it!

> *Oh, fair and lovely Rosalinde,*
> *You have captured my very soul,*
> *Your breath is like the sweetest wind,*
> *Your . . . your true love . . . is*
> *my . . . goal.*

Yes, Flattop! It is a champion verse! I shall seek her out now!" William opened the door, then paused. "Thank you, Flattop. You are a true friend." Then he ran out, pulling the door shut.

True friend. Flattop looked at the closed door and said, "Just remember that."

13

Flattop stood at the entrance to the cookhouse, looking for Alice.

He found chaos instead.

At a nearby table, young girls peeled and sliced apples and pears. Next to them, an old man chopped skinned rabbits and threw the pieces into an iron pot.

"Beg your pardon, my lord." Two muscular men brushed past him carrying a long pole that had three pigs stuck on it.

"Sorry," Flattop mumbled and stepped inside the kitchen.

With a groan, the men hoisted the pole onto metal holders above a big, stone-rimmed barbeque pit.

Flattop wandered over to the pit to watch another man poke at the burning wood with an iron rod. On the flat surface of the grill, chicken halves and slabs of ribs sizzled as they cooked. The smell made Flattop's mouth water. He loved chicken and ribs. Every time his family went to Ed's House O' Ribs, he always ordered the chicken and ribs combo. He vowed to snag both at lunch today.

The man leaned over and pushed the iron rod through the grill to stir the embers below. As he did, sweat dripped from his face onto the cooking food. Flattop winced. Maybe he'd wait until he got home to eat chicken and ribs again.

He walked through a group of ladies who were snapping peas out of their pods, and headed toward the fireplace where a grumpy-looking woman stirred a cauldron with a big wooden spoon. The steam carried the smell of beef stew right to Flattop's nose. His stomach growled as he stood on tiptoe to peek into the bubbling pot. Then he realized the grumpy woman was glaring at him.

"Smells good," he said, forcing a pleasant smile and hoping she wouldn't yell at him.

As he backed away from her, the beef gravy smell was replaced by a pungent odor that stung his eyes. Two teenage girls stood before a huge mound of freshly chopped onions and wiped the tears from their eyes. *They sure could use a food processor in here,* Flattop thought as he blinked and sniffled his way past.

With all this commotion, Alice had to be around. Flattop looked past two men cutting cubes of bacon off a big slab and tossing them into a pot of beans. Sure enough, there was Alice, in her familiar black-and-white dress.

He smiled and ran toward her, but stopped in his tracks. Something was wrong. She sat, head bowed, in the far corner of the cookhouse—turned away from all the activity. He crept up behind her. "Alice?" he said, almost whispering.

She turned around slowly. The rosy pink was gone from her cheeks, and under her green eyes he saw the faintest hint of dark circles. "Good morning, Flattop," she said, smiling weakly.

"What's wrong?" Flattop asked. "Are you sick?"

"No, lad. 'Twas merely a spell of dizziness."

"Is everything okay? I mean—is the baby all right?"

"Yes, lad." Alice placed her hand lightly on her stomach. "I am nearing my time, that is all."

Alarm bells went off in Flattop's head. "Holy cow! You want me to call an ambulance or a doctor or something?"

Alice looked confused. *Of course she's confused!* his mind screamed. *She doesn't know what an ambulance is!* Maybe doctors hadn't even been invented yet. Flattop swallowed hard, then talked in a slow, calm voice. "Do you know what a doctor is?"

"Goodness, yes," Alice said, laughing.

Flattop breathed a sigh of relief. "Well, do you want me to get one for you?"

Alice shook her head. "Do not worry, lad. I will know when it is time." She took hold of Flattop's arm and slowly stood up. "Until then, there is much to do for William's feast."

"Are you sure you should be—"

"M'lady?" The woman who'd been stirring the beef stew curtsied to Alice. "We need some basil and rosemary. And there are serfs at the door to see you."

"Aye," Alice replied, then winked at Flattop. "You see, there is much to do." She reached into a pocket of her dress, pulled out a key and used it to unlock a narrow wooden door. Inside, Flattop could see dried plants hanging upside down from the ceiling and shelves lined with pottery jars.

"What's this?" Flattop asked.

" 'Tis our spice closet," she answered. "Do you not have one in California?"

"Yeah. We call it a pantry." Flattop watched as she cradled the jars in her arm, then shut and locked the door. "And we don't lock it."

"My heavens! Spices are so rare and expensive. How do you keep them safe?" she asked.

Flattop thought for a minute. Did Alice actually mean that people stole spices? In his century, if burglars got in your house, the last thing you'd worry about was whether they ran off with your pepper. "We don't have the problem with . . . spice stealers that you guys do," Flattop said, hoping to close the subject.

"I should like to live in your California," Alice said. She handed the jars to the woman and instructed, "Send the serfs to me." With that, she opened a second door to the bailey.

It would be nice to have Alice for a next-door neighbor. He could teach her how to program a VCR. And with the way she loved to be in the kitchen, she'd probably learn how to make grilled cheese sandwiches and chocolate chip cookies in no time.

Flattop abandoned his daydream when he saw a peasant woman standing at the threshold, clutching a sleeping baby to her chest.

"Mary?" Alice said, smiling. "What is the trouble?"

"If you please, Lady Wickshire." The woman curtsied, then looked at Alice with tear-filled eyes. "My son has not eaten for two days."

Alice put her arm around the woman and guided her to a chair. She extended her arms. "May I hold him?"

Mary handed the boy to Alice.

"How old is he?"

"He has seen one winter."

Alice opened the baby's mouth and stuck her finger inside, rubbing the baby's gums. Suddenly, his eyes flew open and he started crying. Alice held the baby to her, patting him on the back as she swayed back and forth.

Flattop thought about what a great mom Alice would

be to her own baby. Even though the kid would have a creep like James for a father, maybe it would still turn out okay.

When the baby stopped crying, Alice handed him back to Mary, then unlocked the spice closet. She brought out a small jar and a reddish-brown strand of something. "This jar contains a very strong ale. Soak an old scarf in it and let him chew on it. It will relieve the pain."

Mary nodded.

Alice continued, "This is ginger. Sometimes with teeth, a baby's stomach will sour. Boil the ginger into a tea. When it cools, make him drink it. It will settle his stomach."

"Yes, m'lady," Mary said.

Alice helped her to her feet and out the door. "Do not worry. He will soon be well."

A line of serfs had formed at the door, all wanting Alice's medical advice. She cleaned wounds, opened boils, checked infections, and even wrapped a twisted ankle. To some, she gave spices, to others she gave food—to all, she showed warmth and kindness.

"Lady Hemstead wasn't this nice to her serfs," Flattop said.

Alice laughed softly. " 'Tis good business to keep them well. Healthy workers can do more than sick and dying ones."

The last man in line wiped his sleeve across his dirty face, then straightened his ragged, floppy hat. "Beg your pardon, m'lady."

"Henry?"

"Aye, m'lady. I come not for myself. 'Tis my wife, Sarah. She has the fever and has not been able to work the fields for three days."

Alice sat with him and held his hands as he described how the woman was suffering. "The only thing to do is bleed her," Alice told him. "Go to the livery and tell them to ready my cart. You and I shall go to her."

"Aye, m'lady." The man stood up and bowed. "Thank you." He hurried out the door.

Alice pulled a leather bag out of the spice closet, reached inside, and pulled out a small knife. She held it up and inspected it.

"What's that for?" Flattop asked.

"Henry's wife must be bled. I shall need this to make a deep enough cut."

If Flattop had been sitting down, he probably would've fallen off his chair. "You're going to make a sick woman bleed?"

"Aye." She ran the knife across a stone, then touched the edge with her finger.

"Isn't that going to make her sicker?"

"No, lad, bleeding reduces the fever." She placed the knife in the leather bag, along with a couple of pottery jars.

"But sick people need all their blood to help them get better!" he protested, his brain scrambling for proof. Finally he had it. "Look at me," he said. "I've had fevers before. Lots of them. But I always got better. And nobody's ever made me bleed."

She stopped and turned around to look at him closely. Then she gasped. "I almost forgot," she said, reaching into the spice closet and pulling out four strips of red material. "My red cloth."

Flattop shook his head. "Didn't you hear what I said?"

Alice locked the closet door. "Yes, lad. But look at you. Covered in red. 'Tis no wonder you have recovered from your fevers."

"But, Alice—"

She lightly touched his arm. "Flattop, I shall be back in plenty of time to make final preparations for the feast. We shall talk more when I return." She stuck the strips of red cloth into her bag, then left.

Flattop looked around the busy kitchen. "No use hanging around here," he mumbled, then walked outside and stood in the middle of the bailey. Where was the stupid Wizard, anyway? Sighing, he sat down on the cobblestones to feel sorry for himself until Alice got back.

It wasn't long before a group of kids about Margaret's age walked by. They each carried what looked like a wooden top dangling from a piece of yarn. "Hey!" Flattop called. "What're you doing with those?"

The kids exchanged glances. A young girl with braided hair stepped forward and curtsied. "We are spinning, my lord."

"Spinning?"

"Yes, my lord," said one of the boys, holding his hands out so Flattop could get a better look. " 'Tis a drop spindle. It spins yarn for our clothing."

Flattop had seen spinning wheels in fairy tale pictures, but never anything like this. He probably would've let the kids go on their way, but he was curious—and lonely—so he asked them how it worked.

The girl walked in a circle hitting the drop spindle against her thigh. The spindle turned with every step, twisting the yarn tighter and tighter. "This is how it is done," she said. She untied the yarn from the spindle and wound most of it into a ball, which she stashed in her left pocket.

"Cool," Flattop said. "How do you make more?"

The girl reached into the right pocket of her tunic, pulled out a small, fluffy handful of sheep's wool, and separated a chunk. "With this." She tied the remaining length of newly spun yarn on the wooden spindle, then used her fingers to tangle the end of it with the sheep's wool. "You must press very hard to entwine the fleece." Then she walked again, hitting her thigh with the spindle.

Maybe Alison Wedertz would like a sweater made out of wool from the Middle Ages—from her family's castle. That would show her. "Do you knit sweaters and stuff out of this?" he asked.

"No, my lord. We give it to Allan Weaver. He puts it on his loom and makes fabric for our clothes."

Flattop hadn't realized that clothes in 1150 A.D. were made one thread at a time. No wonder even rich people like Alice wore the same thing every day.

"Could I try it?" Flattop asked.

A couple of the kids gasped, and all of them looked uncomfortable. "Y—you are a noble, my lord," the girl stammered. "You do not do such tasks."

"I don't?" Flattop was genuinely disappointed. Being a noble meant he missed out on a lot of fun. He tried a different approach. "Okay, then, I *order* you to let me try it."

The girl curtsied and bowed her head. "As you wish, my lord." She handed him the drop spindle, the ball of yarn, and the sheep's wool.

It took Flattop awhile to get the hang of it, but he was pretty proud of himself when he finally did it right. The children applauded his success.

"We were on our way to watch the knights practice with their squires for tomorrow's tournament," said one of the boys. "Would—would you like to come with us, my lord?"

"Sure," he said, twisting some more sheep's wool into yarn. Maybe he could show William what he'd learned.

14

"Step, step, twist. Step, step twist," Flattop said to himself as he nudged the drop spindle with his right thigh. He followed the kids over the drawbridge.

When they ran ahead of him and disappeared around the outside of the castle, he decided he didn't care. Spinning took time and attention and he wanted to do it right. "Step, step, twist. Step, step—" Flattop looked up.

The land was a richer green than Hemstead. Maybe it was because he was living life as a noble instead of as a peasant this time. Maybe he could appreciate its beauty since he didn't have to work all day in the fields. Whatever the reason, he had to admit that Alison Wedertz's mom came from a nice place.

The distant clanging of metal against metal led him to an open area where a bunch of knights and their squires were fighting with big, heavy swords that took two hands to swing around. Flattop smiled. "Yeah! This is more like it," he said. "This is the *real* Middle Ages."

He saw James right away, dressed in his yellow tunic with the bright blue dragon on the front. He remembered Alice saying James wouldn't fight in the tournament, so

Flattop wondered what he was doing at practice. With a powerful swing, James smashed the flat of his sword into his squire's ribs and sent him rolling to the ground. James laughed as the poor guy curled up into a ball. "Is that all the valor you can muster? How am I to sharpen my skills if you do not offer me a challenge?"

A couple of knights laughed, too, as their squires ran to help James's squire to his feet. Obviously, James was here to show everybody how big and tough he was. Flattop walked away, still looking for William, when he heard James's voice above the clash of swords.

"Well, what have we here? My brother's brave friend, Flattop Kincaid."

Flattop faced James and waved half-heartedly.

James walked over to him, followed by three other knights. "What have you got, lad?" He flashed a menacing grin.

Flattop held out his hand. "It's a drop spindle. I was learning how to—"

James raised his eyebrows and turned to the other knights. "The lad is spinning! The courageous, fearsome Flattop Kincaid is doing women's work!"

Flattop felt his face and ears burn. "Boys do this, too," he said, struggling to keep his anger under control.

"Aye," James said between fits of laughter. "Little boys, fresh from their mother's knee!"

The rest of the knights laughed and nudged each other. Flattop clenched his jaw so hard he thought his teeth would break off. He had a few things to say to James about the way he treated people, but a closer look at all those swords gleaming in the early morning sunlight convinced him to stay quiet.

Flattop wanted to turn around and leave, but his body was frozen with rage. He clutched the drop spindle in one hand and made a fist with the other. James stopped laughing and took a step forward. "Do you not see the humor in—"

"Fear not, Lord Wickshire." A familiar voice rose from the back of the crowd, and William stepped forward. "I shall escort the boy to someplace more suitable. He shall not distract us again."

The boy. The words made a deeper gash in Flattop's heart than James's sword would have. Flattop glared at William, trying to fight the tears that welled in his eyes. "I can take care of myself!" he said, and stomped off as the knights roared with laughter.

Flattop blinked back tears and kept walking. He heard the faint rustling of chain mail and knew William was following him. "Go away!" he ordered.

William ran up beside him. "Flattop, wait! I had to do that."

Flattop glared at him. "Some friend you are."

"James was displeased. He could have tossed you out of the castle—or worse, slapped you in chains."

"I don't care what he does! I'm sick of this stupid place!" Flattop walked faster.

William stopped. "Very well, then. Go. But know this. You are the truest friend I have ever had. I shall miss you."

Flattop tried to keep walking—tried to stay mad—but he felt himself slow to a stop as his mind repeated William's words. *I shall miss you.* Which William should he believe—the one who treated him like a baby, or the one who said, *I shall miss you?* "No, you won't," Flattop mumbled.

"Yes, I shall. I have no one here to help me. No one to listen to me."

Flattop glanced over his shoulder. "You have Alice."

"Alice is just a woman."

"So?"

William sighed and looked away. "Alice has displeased my brother."

"How could she? She runs the whole kitchen and she's nice to everyone. She even helps the serfs and gives them spices. Spices are expensive, you know."

William stood straighter. "She has yet to produce a suitable heir."

"What? You mean have a baby? She's going to have one any day now."

"For her sake, I hope so," William said in a very matter-of-fact voice. "She has lost four. All boys. All born too early. My brother is most unhappy with her."

Flattop shook his head. "You don't think it's her fault, do you?"

" 'Tis her duty, and she has not performed it."

"That's the stupidest thing I ever heard!" Flattop protested. "You can't blame her for—"

" 'Tis her duty, Flattop," William stated again. "And until she produces a live son for my brother, it would be best to distance yourself from her."

"You know what you are?" Flattop charged. "You're a—a pig! And your brother is a—an even bigger pig!"

William shrugged his shoulders. "My brother is Lord Wickshire. I do as he commands. We all do."

"Alice came to your dubbing and James didn't," Flattop reminded him. "You liked her then."

" 'Tis not a question of *liking*." William put his hands on Flattop's shoulders. "She is a sweet-spirited and gentle woman. But we all have our duties to perform. The success of Wickshire depends on that."

Flattop studied William's face. For the first time since

he'd returned to the Middle Ages, he saw truth, sincerity, and kindness there. He remembered his first encounter with William—the gray-hooded squire who thanked Flattop for helping to retrieve his hawk. How could everything have gone so wrong?

Flattop pushed the toe of his cleats into a clump of grass. "It's just that—you're always with those other knights, telling stories and slapping each other on the back and stuff."

"We are knights," William said softly. " 'Tis what we do."

"Well, you could still be nice to people."

William sighed and nodded. "Aye, Flattop. You have my word that I will try."

"And be nice to Alice," Flattop added.

"I will do what I can," William promised. "But I cannot anger my brother."

That wasn't what Flattop wanted to hear, but he knew it was the best William could do. Flattop would just have to look after Alice himself. "Okay."

"Will you stay?" William asked.

"Yeah." Flattop fought the smile forming on his lips. But it felt too good to have the old William back, so he gave up and smiled anyway.

"Most excellent! I go into my first tournament with the grace of God and the devotion of my friend. Now, all I need is the favor of my lady love and I shall be victorious."

Not her again, Flattop thought. "You mean, Rosalinde?"

"Aye," William said, getting that dreamy look in his eyes. "A token of her affection would render me invincible in tomorrow's battle."

"A token?"

"Aye. A small piece of cloth embroidered in her own fair hand would be charm enough." William stood up straight and looked out into the distance, a picture of courage and determination. "I shall ask her today, before the feast in my honor." A devilish smile crossed his lips. "I intend to recite my poem first."

"Uh-huh." Flattop couldn't have cared less, though he hoped she wouldn't laugh at William's poetry. "Well, I gotta go, and you have to practice your fighting. . . ."

"I shall see you at the feast," William said, slapping Flattop on the back. "Wish me good fortune," he said, as he backed away, then turned and ran.

"Good fortune," Flattop said, though it wasn't loud enough for William to hear.

15

"Flattop!" William grabbed Flattop's jacket and pulled him behind the musicians who were playing in the Great Hall. He held up a white handkerchief. "The poem worked! Rosalinde granted me her favor!"

Flattop squinted at the cloth. Tiny flowers of gold thread caught the light from the torches on the wall. "It's kind of shiny."

William rubbed his thumb over one of the yellow flowers. " 'Tis spun gold," he said.

Flattop let out a low whistle. "Wow. I guess you don't blow your nose with that, huh?"

William folded it carefully and tucked it into his sleeve. "I shall treasure this for all my days."

"Uh-huh." Flattop figured a golden handkerchief could probably buy new tires for a BMX bike.

"Tomorrow, when I compete in the tournament, I shall wear it over my heart. And I will dedicate my victories to Rosalinde's fair beauty."

"Uh-huh." It might even buy a whole new bike.

A trumpet sounded and everyone took their seats. Flattop wasn't one of the guests of honor, so he sat in the front row with some of the knights. William sat next to one of the big chairs on the center of the platform, reserved for Lord and Lady Wickshire.

As James and Alice entered the Great Hall, Flattop wondered if Alice had any idea how much trouble she was in. Placing her hand on her stomach, she slowly eased herself into the chair next to William and smiled weakly at him. Flattop was glad to see William smile back.

James sat next to Alice, but his attention was directed to the doorway where Lord Faversham was escorting Rosalinde into the room. Rosalinde looked at William and smiled. William stood and bowed as Rosalinde's father helped her onto the platform. She took the seat next to James and blushed when he kissed her hand.

At a nod from James, the servants filed into the room and placed a thick slice of bread in front of each person. Flattop was so hungry he picked his up to take a bite, then remembered that this was a trencher—a bread plate that was meant to hold his food. At the end of the meal, they would be collected and given to the serfs.

Just thinking about the beef-soaked trenchers he'd eaten when he stayed at John and Ruth's hut made him smile. It'd been a big treat after eating porridge, apple cores, and carrot tops. Flattop decided to make his trencher as delicious as he possibly could for some poor peasant.

He reached for the chicken and ribs, then pulled his hand back when he remembered seeing the cook sweat on them. Instead, he took a steaming hot mound of ham. He put a little bit of stewed rabbit in a corner of his bread. He wasn't going to eat it, but he figured some serf would appreciate it.

As each dish was served, Flattop made a place for it on his trencher. He even squished the boiled onions and watched the juice soak into the bread. The smell of all the food made his mouth water and his stomach growl, so he picked up a handful of ham and ate it.

The meat was tender and tasted salty and sweet at the same time. Next he tried the pears, dripping with honey. His second handful of meat was flavored with the honey still stuck to his fingers. Pretty soon, he was creating new taste sensations by combining all the foods on his trencher. He decided they all tasted pretty good with honey on them.

When the meal was finished, James stood and made a big speech welcoming his brother home to Wickshire. "Sir William," he concluded, " 'tis my heartiest wish to see you prosper in my service. I know I can rely on your courage in the face of danger, your valor in battle, and your loyalty and devotion to me." Even when James was supposed to be honoring William, he was reminding everyone who was in charge.

James asked William to stand. "My brother, tomorrow you join your fellow knights in your first tournament. Though you are young and untried in battle, I have every confidence that you will perform gallantly. However, you shall require an important piece of equipment." James clapped his hands twice. "Bring forth the *great helm*."

A servant entered the room carrying something that looked like a metal bucket. He paused in front of the platform and held it up for everyone to see. There were *oohs* and *aahs* whispered throughout the room. To Flattop, it still looked like a bucket with a rectangular hole cut in the side.

William took the bucket and put it on his head, using the hole to see through.

"Young William," James announced. "Since I am

now in possession of our father's helmet, I give you the *great helm* that was presented to me at my dubbing." James made a sweeping gesture with his hand and the crowd cheered.

William bowed to James and said, "Thank you, Lord Wickshire." But it was hard to understand him since he had a bucket on his head.

James took the great helm off William's head and set it on the chair. "As a knight bound to Wickshire, 'tis fitting for you to have a proper tunic and shield. A display of your heraldry that announces to your enemy that you, Sir William, are sent to do my bidding. Please accept these as my gifts to you on the eve of your first tournament."

A servant entered carrying a green tunic with a white dragon on the front. Another one carried in a brand-new shield that was almost twice as long as an umpire's chest protector. It was green with a white diagonal line running through it. On the bottom half was a white dragon, on the top half, a white star. The two knights sitting across from Flattop nudged each other and looked a little uncomfortable. Flattop guessed they were in awe of William's new equipment and maybe a little afraid to fight him.

William put on the tunic and held the shield in his left hand. James looked out over the rows of tables and shouted, "Lords and ladies, I give you Sir William of Wickshire!" The crowd went nuts, jumping up and down and cheering.

Flattop studied William's face. For a guy with a bunch of new presents he didn't look very happy. In fact, he was forcing a big, fake smile. Flattop looked at Alice. She was standing and applauding, but looking down at the ground. Something was definitely going on, but Flattop didn't have a clue what it was.

William looked at Rosalinde. She stood up, smiled, and applauded with everyone else. They stared at each other for a long time. A *long* time. If this had been a movie, it would've been the scene where the guy and the girl fall in love and Flattop would go to the snack bar for more popcorn.

James glanced at William, then at Rosalinde. "Everybody dance!" he ordered, and the musicians started to play.

The knights pushed past Flattop to congratulate William. In the crush of brightly colored tunics and belted swords, Flattop saw James lead Rosalinde to the dance floor. He looked for Alice on the platform, but she was gone.

Servants were clearing the tables and taking platters of food out the door to the cookhouse. *That's where Alice is,* Flattop thought. She always said the cookhouse was her favorite place. Helping to clear the table like he did at his house on Thanksgiving, he grabbed a platter of ham, dodged through the dancers, and followed the servants out the door. The afternoon sun felt good after being in the dark, smoky castle.

As he walked down the donjon stairs, he decided to ask Alice about William's new green tunic and shield. But first, he'd ask how she was feeling. And how the lady with the fever was doing. And how Alice performed a bleeding on a sick person.

In the cookhouse, he saw lots of servants scraping platters and piling trenchers into a basket in the corner, but Alice wasn't there. He put down the platter of ham and returned to the Great Hall, climbing the stairs two and three steps at a time. Back inside, he leaned against the wall and watched the dancers until his eyes were used to the dark room.

William was dancing with Rosalinde now. They were laughing and looking into each other's eyes again. Flattop thought Alice might be dancing with James, but he was standing alone. Glaring at William.

James whispered something to one of the other knights. The knight nodded and crossed through the dancers to pull William away and congratulate him. James reached for Rosalinde's hand and continued the dance. Flattop felt his stomach turn. James was trying to take Rosalinde away from William. And James was married.

Flattop looked around the room for Alice, but she was nowhere in sight. Sitting in the corner, William's old nurse was tapping her fingers and bobbing her head in time with the music. Flattop walked all the way around the circle—so he wouldn't have to deal with James—and knelt down beside the nurse.

"You may not remember me, but I'm William's friend, and—"

"I remember you," she said, cackling like an old hen. "My beauty is gone, not my brains."

"Well, I was wondering if you knew where Alice was."

"Of course I know."

Flattop waited a moment, but that was all she said. "Well . . . could you tell me where she is?"

"Yes."

Flattop was growing a little impatient with the nurse's game. "Well, then . . . where is she?"

"She is birthing, lad."

"She's what?" Flattop felt his heart pounding in his chest. "Did you call a doctor?"

The old woman cackled again. "Oh my stars! What good would that do? Her midwife is with her."

"What about James? Does he know?"

"Aye, but he would be less help than the doctor." The nurse shook her head. "All we have to do is present him with a son when it is all over."

Flattop thought about James dancing with Rosalinde and his stomach turned again. When he looked back at the dancers, he discovered they both were gone. Flattop charged out the door and down the steps.

He heard a giggle coming from the partially opened doors of the storage room. Sneaking inside, he found sacks like the seed bags John and Ruth had used in the fields at Hemstead, and shelves of large pottery jars and dried meats. One whole wall was lined with wooden barrels.

Flattop heard another laugh—James's—coming from a narrow, dark staircase at the far end of the storeroom. He tiptoed around six butter churns to stand at the top of the stairs.

"Oh, fair Rosalinde, you are the sun and moon to me and I shall love you forever," James said.

"I fear my lord speaks too quickly of love," Rosalinde replied.

"I speak from the heart, fair maid," James insisted.

Flattop felt all the blood leave his brain and a cold sweat break out on his forehead.

James cleared his throat and began to recite,

"If I had but words to bespeak your beauty,
I'd sing songs of birds, fair winds through leaves,
To praise you to the world is my forsworn duty,
When you leave my side, the very soul of me
  grieves."

Flattop wanted to be angry, but he was too disgusted and sick. James, the man who'd never composed a poem for Alice, was making up some pretty fancy stuff for Rosalinde.

James, the man who had just given his brother a big party and a bunch of presents, was stealing his girlfriend.

James, the man who demanded loyalty from everyone, was cheating on Alice while she was upstairs having his baby.

Rosalinde and James had stopped talking. Flattop guessed they were kissing. Unable to take it anymore, Flattop left the storage room and went back to the feast.

The party was still going strong. Everyone was dancing in a circle. Flattop looked for William but didn't see him. He wandered through the Great Hall, getting bumped by the dancers and having ale spilled on him by a drunken knight. The rowdier the party got, the more Flattop was sure he didn't want any part of it.

He grabbed a candle, lit it, and walked up the stone stairs to the upper level of the donjon. A woman with an armload of sheets was about to enter Alice's room.

"Is Alice in there?" Flattop asked.

"Aye," the woman replied.

"Can I see her?"

"Gracious, no!" the woman snapped. "Only women are allowed."

"Is the doctor in there?"

The woman walked back to Flattop. "Did you not hear me, lad? No men allowed. 'Tis not Christian."

Flattop scowled. "What if there's a problem?"

"Should the mother die, the doctor may come in and cut the baby away."

"But—"

"No!" The woman went into the bedchamber, closing the door behind her.

Flattop stared at the closed door. "You'll be okay, Alice," he said quietly, then trudged to his bedchamber. The whole day had gone right in the trash, and he'd been powerless to stop it. When he opened his chamber door, he saw a candle flickering inside. William's shadowy figure sat slumped on the bed.

"What are you doing here?" Flattop asked. "You're the guest of honor at the party."

William sighed. "I needed to keep counsel with myself." He rubbed the top of his new shield. "Things have not gone as I expected," he said.

"You can say that again," Flattop agreed. After a moment of silence, he added, "Alice is having her baby."

"Aye."

"They won't let me visit her."

"Of course. 'Twould not be Christian."

"So I heard." Now it was Flattop's turn to sigh. "Hey, what was going on out there today—I mean, with your tunic and shield and everything."

William turned the shield toward Flattop. "Did you not see? 'Tis green."

"So?"

"Green is unlucky. It stands for pleasure . . . for youth." He traced the white star with his finger. "My brother has stated to the world that I am childish and a pleasure-seeker. These are not knightly qualities."

"Neither is cheating on your wife, but James is doing it."

William raised his head. "What?"

Flattop realized he'd have to tell William about Rosalinde. If his friend was having a bad day before, it was about to get a whole lot worse. "You're not the only one writing poetry for Rosalinde. Your brother is, too. And his is better."

William sat motionless on the bed. "Oh."

"Is that it? *Oh?* He's stealing your girlfriend!"

William pulled his hand in and out of the leather strap on the back of the shield. "Rosalinde is not my . . . girlfriend, as you call it. She is my inspiration."

"What?"

"She inspires me to do well in battle. That is all."

Flattop frowned. "That's not true, and you know it!"

" 'Tis but courtly love, Flattop. I seek not a wife. I merely seek her favor to give me heart in battle."

Flattop shook his head. "She's your girlfriend."

William looked like he'd just lost the World Series. "And James is Lord Wickshire."

16

"Wizard? Are you there?" Flattop stood on the very top of the donjon, under a million twinkling stars. He rubbed the dark glass across his thigh, then looked up. The crescent moon was so thin it looked like a fingernail clipping. He positioned the glass to reflect what little moonlight there was. "Wizard, I need to talk to you."

The glass grew lighter in color, then flickered. In between the pale flashes of light, a faint outline of the Wizard began to form. Flattop held the glass up closer to his eyes. "Wizard! Come in, Wizard!"

A muffled voice replied, "I'm trying, my boy. Be patient."

"Okay . . . but hurry up!"

Even through the flickering image, Flattop could see the Wizard raise one eyebrow. "Is that your idea of patience?"

"I'm sorry, but I gotta know something."

The Wizard yawned. "Shouldn't you be in bed? What time is it?"

Flattop held up his watch and pushed the button to light the numbers. "Midnight." He positioned the glass to reflect the moon again.

The Wizard rubbed his eyes. "For goodness sakes,

my boy, how am I supposed to get my beauty sleep when I have to attend to you around the clock?''

"I haven't even talked to you since I got here!"

"That doesn't mean I haven't been with you."

Flattop tilted his head. "You've been with me? Where?"

"Here and there. Right under your nose until yesterday."

Flattop scowled. Right under his nose? He quickly reviewed everywhere he'd gone—the town, the Hart's Blood Inn, Quentin's monastery, the castle, tournament practice, the—

"Well, my boy," the Wizard said, interrupting Flattop's thoughts, "do you have something to discuss, or may I go back to sleep?"

"No!" Flattop answered. "I mean, yes! I mean, don't go. I want to know about Alice."

"What about her?"

"Her baby. Does she get a boy?"

The Wizard stroked his long, white beard. "Now, why do you want to know that?"

"Because she's in big trouble with James. She has to have a son and it has to live or he'll—" Flattop didn't actually know what James would do. "Or he'll do something bad to her . . . I think."

"I see. So I should predict the future for you now?"

"Yeah." Even though Flattop said it with confidence, the whole idea suddenly sounded stupid.

"My boy, I can't tell you what's going to happen. It's against the rules of the game."

"You did it before."

The Wizard shook his head. "I've explained things to you. That's different. You ask questions and I answer them."

Flattop brightened. "Okay, I've got a question."

"What is it?"

"Is Alice going to be okay?"

The Wizard folded his arms across his chest. "You're not playing fair, Marvin."

"Okay, okay," Flattop grumbled. "I'll ask something else." He thought for a moment. "Why won't they let the doctor in to see Alice?"

"Good heavens, Flattop! He's a man! It wouldn't be Christian."

Flattop kicked his cleat against the stone floor. "That's what everybody says!"

"Well, it's true. People in the Middle Ages don't see the opposite sex undressed. It's a sin."

Flattop thought about all the movies in his century where actors took off their clothes. Things had certainly changed. "Even doctors can't see someone undressed?" He wanted to make sure.

The Wizard shrugged. "Welcome to medieval times."

"Medieval?"

"Yes, my boy. Medieval. It means in the middle. As in, *Middle Ages*."

"Ohhhh." Flattop remembered hearing the word once before, when a bunch of guys dressed up like knights rode horses in a parade. They called themselves The Medieval Brothers. But they seemed nice. Nothing like James, who . . . Flattop held the glass closer to his face. "Wizard! James is trying to get Rosalinde to be his girlfriend."

"I know."

"Well . . . what's going to happen?"

The Wizard frowned, then cleared his throat.

"Oh. The future. Sorry." Flattop's brain scrambled for a suitable question. "Why is James such a creep?"

"It's a different time, Flattop. People think differently—have different values. Have you heard of people who are psychic?"

"Sure. They read minds and stuff."

"In medieval times, they were charged with witchcraft, then tortured and killed."

Flattop held the dark glass away from his face. "Well, that's just plain stupid."

"It's not up to you to judge, my boy. Your only task is to learn."

Flattop sighed. "Well, I learned I want to go home."

"Very well," the Wizard said. "Catch me."

Flattop felt his cheeks get hot. "How can I? You're never around!"

"Yes, I am. You haven't been looking."

The glass hissed and sputtered, and the picture got snowy like a TV with no antenna. "Wizard!" Flattop repositioned the glass, but no amount of adjusting could bring it back.

The Wizard was gone.

Flattop picked up the candle he'd left inside the door and walked back down toward his bedchamber. True, he hadn't really looked for the Wizard lately. But he'd been a little busy having an *adventure*. Flattop stopped halfway down the tiny staircase and smiled to himself. A *medieval* adventure. In Alison Wedertz's castle.

Boy, would she be jealous if she knew.

He opened the door to the bedchamber and walked inside. William was sound asleep on his side of the bed. His chain mail was carefully draped over one of the wooden chests. Flattop walked over and ran his hand across the thousands of linked metal rings. *It must've*

112

taken somebody a really long time to make this, he thought.

Underneath the chain mail was William's bright green tunic with the white dragon sewn in the front. On the floor, his new shield lay face down next to his great helm. Flattop glanced at William, making sure he was still asleep, then he knelt down, picked up the shield and held the candle closer.

The white, winged dragon matched the one on William's tunic. Flattop ran his thumb across the green star in the upper corner. Nice workmanship for something that was meant to be an insult.

Green. Who would've thought a color could be—

"Flattop?"

William's sleepy voice startled Flattop and he jumped to his feet. "I—I was just—looking at your—your shield."

"I can see that."

Flattop had never touched any of William's knight stuff before. And now, the one time he did, he got caught. He tried to make conversation. "Nice dragon."

" 'Tis the symbol of Wickshire," William said, still resting his head on the pillow.

Flattop sighed with relief. At least William didn't look like he was going to jump out of bed and beat him up. "Nice star."

William turned his head the other way and pulled the covers up over his shoulder. "It means I am the third-born son of Wickshire."

"But you're the second—"

William rolled back once more. "My brother Andrew, remember?"

"Oh." Flattop winced. First, he's caught messing around with William's shield, then he brings up the subject of dead brothers. "I forgot about Andrew. I mean, I didn't forget, I—"

"Flattop, please. My first tournament is tomorrow. I need to sleep."

"Oh, sure." Flattop shrugged. "No problem." He laid the shield down and blew out the candle, plunging the room into total darkness. With his hands out in front of him, he shuffled over to the bed, hoping he wouldn't stub his toe or fall down or anything.

He untied his cleats, eased into the bed, and pulled the covers over him. *Green,* he thought. *Why did James have to give him green?* Flattop always thought he had it bad being stuck with a sister like Marcia. But James was worse. "William? I'm sorry you got green stuff."

William didn't answer. He was probably asleep.

It was probably just as well.

17

Flattop woke to the sound of the chamber door closing. William's tunic and shield were gone—and so was William. *He must've gone to the tournament,* Flattop thought as he rubbed the sleep out of his eyes.

The tournament!

Flattop sat up, put on his cleats, and double-knotted the laces. He ran his hands through his hair, then picked up his baseball cap, which was wedged between his pillow and the wall.

He had no idea when the tournament would begin, but things got started pretty early in the Middle—in *medieval* times. Flattop smiled. He liked the sound of his new word. Pulling the baseball cap down onto his forehead, he ran out the door.

He stopped outside Alice's chamber door, hoping to ask how she was, but no one was around. He almost knocked on the door, but decided to come back later. "Hope you're okay," he mumbled to the closed door, then ran down the steps to the Great Hall.

Most of the knights were just waking up after sleeping on the big wooden tables, and their squires were crawling out from blankets on the floor. Flattop's shoes crunched through the rushes. He was glad he got to sleep in a bed instead of a pile of sticks and leaves that were filled with fleas, lice, and the bones from last night's dinner.

Across the room, Flattop saw William talking to Philip, the kid who had showed them to their room when they first arrived.

Flattop stared at the way the blazing white dragon stood out on William's green tunic. Maybe green wasn't the best color a knight could wear into battle, but William looked pretty good in it. He looked older and more powerful than he had as a gray-hooded squire at Hemstead.

William waved at him. "Flattop! Come join us."

Flattop walked across the Great Hall, careful not to step on any squires.

"Flattop Kincaid," William said, "I present to you my newly appointed squire, Philip."

Flattop wasn't sure if he should say "Pleased to meet you" or "Congratulations," so he just said, "Hi."

Philip looked at William with a puzzled expression. William shrugged. "He's from California."

Feeling his cheeks get warm with embarrassment, Flattop tried to make better conversation. "So . . . you're a squire."

Philip smiled. "I am honored to be in the service of Sir William of Wickshire. Especially on the day of his first tournament."

"Yeah. It's pretty exciting all right," Flattop said.

"Philip and I are going to practice before the competition," said William. "Would you like to join us?"

Flattop winced. That last practice he'd tried to watch ended up in a big fight. He shook his head. "Nah. You need to concentrate. You know, get into your game."

William nodded, but Flattop could see he was confused.

"Besides, I want to check on Alice."

"Very well," William said. "I shall see you at the tournament." He leaned in to whisper, "Remember, I am dedicating today's victories to Rosalinde."

"Uh-huh," Flattop replied.

As William and Philip walked out the door, Flattop shook his head in disbelief. William was acting like he hadn't heard a word about James trying to steal Rosalinde.

Hopeless.

As he trudged up the stairs toward Alice's room, Flattop heard giggling and whispers. He looked up to see Rosalinde in her red satin dress coming down the stairs, surrounded by servant girls. Flattop stepped to the side and watched them pass. William was right. Rosalinde was pretty. And graceful. And very friendly to the servants. Her long, dark hair was decorated with flowers and ribbons, and gently swayed as she walked.

Suddenly, Flattop yelled, "Hey, Rosalinde!"

The giggling stopped, and all the girls looked back at him with open-mouthed gasps.

Shocked at what he'd done, Flattop felt his heart pounding in his chest. What now? He cleared his throat. "William really likes you."

The light in the stairway wasn't very good, but Flattop thought he saw her blush. "He may not write very good poems, but he's a nice guy." Flattop paused a moment, then added, "And he's not married, or anything."

Rosalinde smiled.

"He's dedicating his wins to you, because you inspire him."

Rosalinde's dark brown eyes seemed to ask for more.

But Flattop was out of words. He shoved his hands

in his pockets and shrugged his shoulders. "That's it, I guess. I just wanted you to know."

Rosalinde stood perfectly still for a moment, then curtsied and said softly, "Thank you, my lord." She turned, joined the servant girls, and they all scampered down the steps.

Flattop leaned against the cool, stone wall and let out a long breath of air. He took off his hat and wiped his brow with the red sleeve of his tee shirt. This girl stuff was difficult.

He was almost back to normal by the time he reached Alice's bedchamber, where two women paced outside.

"How's Alice?" he asked. "Has she had the baby yet?"

"No, lad," one of them said.

"It's been a long time now, hasn't it?"

The women looked at each other. One leaned against the heavy wooden door and rubbed her forehead. The other walked over to Flattop and put her arm around his shoulder. "The baby is turned. 'Twill take the midwife some time to get it into the proper position."

Flattop fought the feeling of dread deep in his stomach. "She'll be okay, though. Right? I mean, she'll live, won't she?"

The woman sighed and patted his shoulder. "Aye, lad. Her chances are good. As long as the midwife can do her work."

"And the baby?"

"We do not know. A baby that cannot be righted . . . We simply do not know."

Flattop fought the tears that welled in his eyes. Why Alice? She never hurt anybody. She never said a mean thing. Never made fun of anybody. All she needed was a healthy baby boy. That's all.

118

"Where's James?" Flattop asked, hearing the bitterness in his own voice. "He should be here."

"Goodness, Lord Wickshire has no part in this. We shall tell him when it is all over."

Figures, Flattop thought. He sniffed and rubbed his hand across his nose.

"Lad?" the woman said softly.

"I'm okay," he grumbled. "Just—could you tell Alice that—tell her Flattop Kincaid says . . . hello."

The woman took Flattop's hand and squeezed it. "Yes, lad. I shall tell her. Now, why don't you run along to the tournament and let us attend to our duties."

"I'll stay here. Alice may need me, and—"

"No, lad. Go to the tournament. All the young men and ladies are there now. Go and enjoy yourself."

Flattop could tell by the woman's steely gaze that there would be no convincing her. "All right," he agreed. "I'll go. But I won't have any fun because I'll be worried about Alice the whole time."

She smiled and patted his hand again. "Try to have fun. Leave this work to us, as Lord Wickshire and the doctor have."

Flattop headed downstairs toward the Great Hall. "Stupid ladies!" He took off his cap and smacked it on the stone wall. "Stupid! Stupid! Stupid!"

It's not up to you to judge, my boy. The Wizard's words echoed in his brain.

Flattop froze in place. "Wizard?"

Nothing.

He took out the dark glass and looked at it.

Nothing.

He moved closer to one of the torches on the wall, so the glass reflected the firelight.

Something.

A faint image of the Wizard began to appear. Flattop gasped. "It *is* you!" He held the glass closer to his face. "Wizard, Alice is having trouble with the baby. What can I do to help?"

"Go to the tournament."

"I can't! What if something happens to her baby?"

"What if it does? Can you stop it?"

Flattop scowled. "Well, no."

"Can you help her?"

"Nobody'll let me," Flattop snapped.

"Then go to the tournament."

"But I—"

"Marvin, my boy, this matter is out of your hands. There is nothing you can do here. But at the tournament, a newly dubbed knight will need all the friends he can get."

Flattop thought for a moment. "You mean, William?"

The Wizard rolled his eyes. "What is it you say? Oh, yes. *Duh!*"

Flattop glared into the glass.

"You can make a difference at the tournament." The Wizard whispered, "William needs to see that he has friends, especially today."

Flattop leaned against the wall, watching black smoke curl upward from one of the wall torches. If he couldn't trust the Wizard, who could he trust? "Okay," he said. "I'll go to the tournament."

The Wizard smiled. "There's a good lad," he said as he faded from view.

"Yeah, right," Flattop grumbled as he headed for the tournament field. "Useless, but good."

18

The square, fenced-in tournament field was located on the back side of the castle. It was smaller than Flattop had imagined—about half the size of a football field— and it looked like a big horse corral. Serfs crowded around the fence to get a better view. Children pushed to the front and clung to the wooden railings.

At one end, a tall platform with a cloth roof kept James, Lord Faversham, and Rosalinde out of the morning sun. They sat calmly drinking ale while servants bustled around behind them.

A man with a long-necked trumpet stood by James, and another stood by Rosalinde. Each horn displayed a yellow banner with the royal blue dragon of Wickshire on both sides.

The trumpets sounded. A gate opened and the first of the knights rode in, followed by his squire. The rest of the knights and squires entered and circled the tournament field. Each knight wore a tunic with his own colors and symbols, and each squire carried a flag with a matching design. The designs were not only pictures of brightly colored dragons, but lions, eagles, deer, and a funny-looking animal with the head and wings of an eagle and the body of a lion. One of the serfs called it a griffin.

Flattop squeezed through the crowd of peasants to get a better look. His red satin jacket made them step quickly aside. Even though they gave him lots of room, Flattop could still smell them—smoky and unwashed.

As each knight passed by, the adults cheered and the little kids waved. It reminded Flattop of a circus parade. He stepped up on the lowest railing of the fence and craned his neck to see. At last, William entered the tournament field, riding stick-straight and proud.

"Hey, William!" Flattop shouted.

William looked around until he found Flattop, then smiled and waved. Maybe the Wizard was right. William looked really happy to see him.

"Good luck, okay?"

William gave him an even bigger smile and nodded. "Thank you, my friend."

My friend. Flattop grinned. Things were looking up.

William continued around the circle, then stopped in front of James and bowed his head. James nodded in return. When William rode in front of Rosalinde, she applauded. Lord Faversham and James looked at her, then scowled at each other.

Flattop was pleased with himself. Talking to Rosalinde hadn't been easy, but now he was glad he had done it.

The knights finished their slow circle, then formed two lines facing each other and dismounted. The squires led the horses away and returned on foot a few minutes later carrying bundles of swords, helmets, and extra shields. Each squire leaned the weapons against the fence behind his knight.

The knights in one line viciously glared at the knights in the opposing line. Even William looked like he was ready to kill someone. Flattop had only seen mad-dog

122

stares like that on pro football players just before the ball was snapped.

James welcomed all the nobles and introduced his honored guests—Lord Faversham and Rosalinde. Then, he held his goblet high in the air and toasted the brave knights.

The squires gave helmets to their knights, then ran back and stood by the fence. Flattop watched William adjust the bucket-shaped great helm on his head. William had looked kind of stupid wearing it the day before, but now that he stood in the field with a bunch of other bucket-heads, he fit in.

Flattop was glad the knights had designs on their shields and tunics. Without them, no one would know who they were fighting. He looked down at his baseball shirt. When he played in a game, his uniform let everyone in the stands know whose side he was on, just like a dragon told everyone that William was from Wickshire.

When James called for the field marshal, a tough-looking older guy stepped up to the platform. He announced, ''In the name of God and St. Michael, do your battle!''

With a roar, the knights charged forward and started beating each other up. Broadswords clanged and thudded. Heavy steel blades bashed shields and helms. Flattop's mouth dropped open. Where was the jousting? Where were the games of skill? This was worse than football. Worse than boxing. This was war.

The crowd cheered and pushed hard against the fence. Flattop climbed up another railing to look for William's green-and-white tunic. He found his friend just as William swung his broadsword against another knight's thigh.

''Go for it, William!'' Flattop shouted.

The knight fell to the ground and William continued his attack, knocking the sword out of the knight's hand.

"Yes!" Flattop raised his fist in the air.

William picked up the broadsword and held it out to the marshal, who nodded.

Rosalinde applauded.

James frowned.

Philip ran in and took the newly won sword back to his position on the fence. As the defeated knight struggled to his feet, his squire rushed forward with another sword.

William found a new battle with a knight dressed in navy blue. *Indigo,* Flattop remembered. Like Blanche's tunic at the Hart's Blood Inn. As he watched William deflect a blade with his shield, Flattop remembered how William had stayed up all night at the inn, drinking ale and telling his big stories.

William might be conceited, but he seemed to be a good enough fighter to back it up. The indigo knight ended up on the ground. His helm fell off and he let go of his shield. William picked up both items, held them up to the marshal, then gave them to Philip.

"Way to go, Willie baby!" Flattop yelled.

Rosalinde applauded again.

James sat back and glared at William.

Watching William defeat his opponents was fun—for about an hour. Then Flattop started to get bored. Oh sure, there had been some blood—that was pretty cool. And one knight was dragged off the field, unconscious. But Flattop's enthusiasm didn't last.

He still shouted encouragement to William, but he often found himself watching other knights or just looking at people in the crowd. The squires kept busy bringing out new weapons or wrapping their knights' wounds.

A knight who got too tired would limp back to his squire and rest. The squire would give him some food and ale and point to the knights who were doing the best.

But the whole thing went on too long. Now Flattop understood why boxing matches and football games were timed. A person can only take so much fighting. After almost three hours, Flattop saw William trudge over to the sidelines and sit down.

Flattop walked around the fence, squeezing his way through the crowd until he got close to his friend. "Hey, William!" he shouted as he climbed the fence and draped his arms over the top railing. "You're doing pretty good."

William looked at his growing collection of battle gear he'd won from his competitors and smiled. "Aye! It'll fetch a pretty ransom when I sell it back to the owners."

"You don't get to keep it?"

"I could, but 'tis the practice of the tournament to allow each knight a chance to buy back the things lost from him in battle."

Flattop reached down and touched the big red-and-blue jewels on the handle of a broadsword. "Bet this one costs a fortune."

William nodded. "Aye. Sir Richard's. 'Twas his father's, and his father's before him. It will be a matter of family honor to buy it back from me."

Flattop wondered what it would be like to lose a Little League game and have to give up his bat and glove—and then buy them back. It didn't sound like a very good deal.

William tore into a chunk of salted meat. "There are

many worthy opponents on the field. I thank God that my skills are strong.''

''Who decided what team you'd fight for?'' Flattop asked.

''Team?''

Flattop nodded. ''Yeah, you all came in and stood in two lines . . . you know . . . before you started bashing each other around.''

''That is a tournament line. It has no purpose except to keep us from fighting before the field marshal commands it.'' William took a swig of ale, then wiped the sweat from his forehead. ''Our first opponent must be from the other side of the line. After that, 'tis every man for himself.''

Flattop saw a couple more knights leave the field to rest. ''So . . . when will this be over?'' He tried his best to sound curious, not bored.

William looked into the afternoon sky. ''About sunset.''

''What?'' That meant another two or three hours of watching knights bash each other around.

''At the end of the tournament, we will tally up our newly seized equipment, and the knights with the highest numbers will win prizes.''

Flattop was glad there was some point to all this. ''What kind of prizes?''

William shrugged. ''Fish, a new helm, a saddle, or a bolt of Lady Wickshire's finest cloth.''

All this fighting to win a fish? Flattop felt a twinge of guilt for leaving Alice's door. Maybe when William went back onto the field, he'd sneak away and check on her.

''Flattop!'' William stood up. ''Look!''

Flattop followed William's gaze up to the tall platform where Rosalinde sat on the edge of her chair, gazing at William. William raised his hand toward her. She stood and waved a red scarf.

William sighed. "Is she not the fairest creature in all the world?"

"Uh-huh." Flattop rolled his eyes. Then he noticed that Lord Faversham and James were watching William's every move.

And they didn't look happy.

"Hey, William. Maybe you'd better not be looking at her right now. You've got a tournament to fight."

"Aye, my friend. But I do not know how to tear my eyes away from her beautiful face."

Flattop glanced at the two men again. "Well, try."

"I am her humble and devoted servant." William bowed his head and knelt toward Rosalinde.

Rosalinde clutched her scarf to her chest and smiled.

Lord Faversham pulled his daughter back into her seat, as James looked on.

William put on his great helm with a big flourish, grabbed his sword, and strode back onto the field. No sooner had he begun to fight when the trumpets sounded. Everyone looked up to see James standing on the platform holding a great helm and a yellow shield with a blue dragon.

The crowd quieted and looked up to the platform. James announced, "Lords and ladies, a love of battle skills is part of the great heritage my brother and I share. On the celebration of his dubbing, I find I can no longer sit as a spectator. Therefore, I relinquish the duties of overseer to Lord Faversham and happily join the games."

The knights raised their swords and cheered.

"I have requested a favor of the beautiful Lady Rosalinde and she has granted it to me."

The crowd went wild as Rosalinde, prompted by a glare from her father, walked to James and handed him her red scarf. James kissed her hand and climbed down to the tournament field, stuffing the scarf inside his tunic.

William stood on the field with his sword and shield by his side. He stared at Rosalinde, but she turned away.

Once James entered the contest, the fight resumed with new energy. James began beating up guys right and left. Every time he did, he would look at Rosalinde and bow. She would politely smile back.

Flattop clutched the top railing of the fence, his knuckles turning white. He could see that James was choosing opponents closer and closer to William. William continued to fight gallantly, seizing a shield and two more broadswords in the process.

Finally, the brothers were face-to-face. Now Flattop understood why James was at tournament practice yesterday. He'd planned this duel all along. The brothers stalked in a circle, each waiting for the other to attack. Then James's sword came down with a powerful crack on William's shield. William swung his sword from around the side, but James's shield deflected it. From the sound of the clashing metal and wood, both of them meant business.

James faked a sideways assault. As William moved his shield to meet it, James switched directions and bashed William's helmet with a *clank.*

Flattop gasped and held his ears in sympathy. The noise inside that bucket helmet must've been deafening. William staggered backward. James made a couple of fancy moves with his broadsword, then lunged forward and slammed it into William's ribs. Next, with a slicing blow to the opposite leg, James sent William to his knees.

The knights standing nearest to the brothers stopped fighting and backed away, giving them lots of room.

William rolled onto his back and laid his shield across his ribs. He raised his sword and turned away James's next thrust. But he was so intent on scrambling to his feet, he didn't see James's sword swing down across his knee. Flattop heard William cry out.

That's when he realized that *all* the fighting had stopped and everyone was quietly watching the contest.

"Come on, William!" Flattop shouted. "You can do it!"

James pushed his shield into his brother's chest and shoved him on his back. William tried to raise his sword again, but James knocked it out of his hand and kicked him in the chest.

"Where is your courage now, little brother?" James taunted.

William scooted backward, using his shield to protect against the constant sword blows. When he finally reached his weapon, he swung it with all his might, catching James in the ankle.

James roared like a wounded animal. "You ungrateful varlet! I will show you what it takes to be a knight!" With that, he clutched the broadsword handle and swung it with all the power of a home-run hitter. William had been able to get to his knees, but the force of the sword on his shield toppled him again.

"Get up, William!" Flattop yelled. "Get up!"

James struck another blow to his brother's ribs. William doubled over, trying to hide as much of his body beneath his shield as he could. James sliced the sword across William's calf. William pulled his leg farther up under the shield.

"Come on, Sir William! Lady Rosalinde wants to see a battle!" James shouted.

Flattop glanced at Rosalinde, who was peeking at the battle between her fingers.

With a sudden move, William rolled over on his back and swung his shield into James's hip. James limped backward and William got to his feet.

"Get him, William!" Flattop shouted.

William swung the broadsword at James's head, but James defended himself with his shield.

"Swing it, Willie! Swing, batter batter! Swing!" Flattop saw Philip turn his head and stare at him, confused. "We say that in California when we have a . . . a tournament," Flattop explained.

"I think we need to end this, dear brother," James said with a sneer. He charged forward. William had no choice but to back up. A blow to the right side of William's great helm was followed by a blow to the left. William paused for a moment and James lunged forward and pushed him down.

He kicked his younger brother's shield away, then slashed at his arm until William dropped his sword. He threw his own shield aside, and using both hands to grip his sword, came down on the great helm as though he held an axe. The loud clash of metal on metal made everyone gasp. William lay motionless, with James standing over him trying to catch his breath.

"There we are, little brother. Now *that* was a contest." James walked over to retrieve William's sword and shield. He held it up to the field marshal, who nodded. "I claim these in the name of Lady Rosalinde.

May her grace and beauty continue to be an inspiration.'' He bowed to her.

She lowered her head.

William began to stir. He tried to sit up.

James circled around his brother. "Sir William fought bravely today. And while his skills may be lacking, there is much he will learn in my service." He stood back and ordered, "Arise, William of Wickshire."

William tried to get up but couldn't. Philip ran to his side. Flattop bounded over the top of the fence and followed. They each took one of William's arms and helped him stand.

"William," Flattop whispered. "Are you all right?"

"Aye," came the strained whisper from inside the helm.

"My lords and ladies," James announced, "I know it is customary for the knight victorious to ransom his winnings." He held William's sword and shield up again for the crowd to see. "But William is my brother and has proved to be a noble warrior. As a tribute to his valiant effort today, I humbly return them as a gesture of family loyalty and brotherly love." With that, James knelt before William and offered up the sword and shield.

For a moment, William stood motionless. Then he took his sword and shield.

The crowd cheered wildly. "Long live Wickshire! Long live Wickshire!" James returned to his original position on the tall platform and pulled the red scarf out of his tunic. He kissed it and handed it back to Rosalinde, who smiled and curtsied.

James looked out over the tournament field and announced, "Let the games continue!"

The broadswords clashed once again, and Flattop and Philip escorted William off the tournament field.

19

Flattop sat in the blacksmith's barn watching the big, sweaty man pound the great helm so William could get his head out. When the blacksmith finally removed the great helm, Flattop was shocked to see that William's nose was bloody and crooked and he had two black eyes.

"William!" Flattop said. "Your face is a mess."

"Your nose is broken, my lord," the blacksmith said.

Flattop looked around the barn. "Don't you have a washcloth or something?"

"I do," William answered, grimacing in pain as he reached through the neckline of his tunic. He pulled out the handkerchief Rosalinde had given him and handed it to Flattop.

Flattop looked at the fine gold thread that ran through it. "It's going to get all bloody," he warned.

William looked down and sighed. " 'Tis of no consequence."

Flattop saw a bucket of water the blacksmith used to cool red-hot irons. He dipped the cloth in the dirty water then held it out. "Here. Don't rub too hard."

William winced as he dabbed the dried blood off his skin. His eyes began to water and he started to sniffle.

"It stings," he mumbled. Once his face was cleaned off, he stared at the handkerchief as if deciding what to do with it, then he put it back inside his tunic.

"You're keeping that?" Flattop asked. "After what she did to you?"

William shrugged, then caught his breath at the pain it must've caused. "Rosalinde did nothing but be beautiful."

Flattop started to argue, then realized it would be pointless. "Whatever," he said with a sigh.

Turning for the door, William gasped for air. He said his chest hurt so badly he couldn't breathe. Flattop had seen a TV show about a stuntman who cracked his ribs, then fastened a couple of tight leather belts around the sore spots and went back to work.

Deciding that leather belts were worth a try, he and Philip helped William walk to the livery, where they tied some horse reins around William's chest. He said it made a big difference. He even half-smiled.

Flattop and Philip helped William to his room. As they passed the Great Chamber, Flattop asked a woman about Alice. "She's resting," was the reply.

"Did she . . . ?" Flattop felt so silly asking the same question, he couldn't even finish his sentence.

"Aye, lad."

If he hadn't been holding William, Flattop probably would've jumped up and down. "All right! Way to go!"

" 'Tis a baby girl."

Flattop felt his heart sink to his knees, and it made him feel shaky all over. "Wh—what?"

"A girl," the woman repeated.

He looked to William for comfort, but William just shook his head. Grinding the heel of his cleat into a crack on the floor, Flattop asked, "Is—is she okay? Alice, I mean?"

"Aye lad, both she and the baby are fine. But Lady Wickshire has had a difficult birth. She will need time to recover."

"Sure. I understand." William tugged at him to leave. "Will you tell her that Flattop Kincaid says . . ." He thought for a moment. "Congratulations."

"That I will, lad."

Flattop turned to help William down the hall to his chamber. Once inside, they got William undressed and eased him into the bed. Philip left to fetch a strong ale for William.

Flattop sat on the bed. "This is your brother's fault, you know."

"No. 'Tis mine." William groaned as he tried to change positions in the bed. "I knew he was interested in Rosalinde."

"What's that got to do with anything? He's married."

"He is Lord Wickshire. He may do what he chooses." William took a series of shorter breaths. "But she favored me so highly today. I thought James no longer wanted her."

Flattop could've sworn his heart stopped beating. Rosalinde was flirting with William because of what Flattop had told her. *William really likes you.*

He glanced at his friend. Battered face, broken nose, black eyes, cracked ribs. All because Flattop butted in. William was disgraced in front of the girl he loved because Flattop couldn't keep his stupid mouth shut. William's injuries weren't James's fault. They were Flattop's.

If he was half as brave as he thought he was, he'd confess what he'd done. Flattop looked down and rubbed the bottom snap on his red satin jacket between his thumb and forefinger. *Tell him,* his conscience directed.

"You know, William . . . I think I know why Rosalinde acted that way."

William looked up at Flattop. "So do I, my friend."

Flattop felt sweat break out on his upper lip. "You do?"

"Aye. She is a woman and cannot control her thoughts or deeds. Why did I not realize it sooner?" William shook his head. "Poor, sad creature."

Flattop paused. What good would confessing do now? After all, William already had a satisfactory explanation, even if it made no sense. He took another second to make sure his conscience didn't mind *not* confessing. Nope. He was off the hook.

Besides, the poor guy had lost Rosalinde and been clobbered by his older brother. The last thing he needed to hear was that his friend had caused the whole thing. Flattop stood up and cleared his throat. "Well, I'd better let you get some rest."

William tried to raise his head. "Do you see my great helm?"

Flattop looked around the room. "No."

"I believe I left it in the livery. Would you mind fetching it for me? 'Twas a gift from Lord Wickshire."

A good reason to lose it, Flattop thought. "Okay, I'll get it for you."

He pulled the door closed and walked down the dark hallway until he came to Alice's room.

"Is she still resting?" he asked the woman standing by her door.

"Aye," she said softly.

Flattop nodded and walked down to the Great Hall.

The rüstling of his cleats through the rushes echoed off the stone walls of the big, empty room. He realized he felt just as empty. Alice had a baby girl, James had impressed Rosalinde, and William had a friend who helped him get beaten up.

Could things get any worse? He sighed. Only if he stayed here longer.

He pushed open the heavy, wooden door and walked down the donjon steps. It was definitely time to go home. But where was the Wizard?

Right under your nose until a couple days ago. Really? Under his nose? Flattop crossed his eyes and looked at his nose. What did the Wizard mean?

As he made his way to the livery, he tried to figure out how the old man could've been right under his nose. He finally shrugged it off, deciding the Wizard was being uncooperative.

He opened the stable door and looked at the piles of hay and the leather reins, but he couldn't find the helmet. He heard a hollow metal sound followed by a horse's whinny. When he walked down to investigate, he found the horse he'd ridden from Hemstead.

"Hello, horse," Flattop said, stepping up on the bottom rail. Maybe he should name it. Nah. He was going home as soon as he caught the Wizard.

The horse lowered its head and pushed something through the straw. It hit the back of the stall with a *clunk*.

"What've you got?" Flattop asked, climbing up to the next railing.

Clunk.

Flattop saw a glint of metal. He jumped into the stall and brushed the straw away to reveal William's great helm. "Hey! Thanks!" He patted the horse on the head.

That's when he looked into the horse's eyes.

Wizard eyes.

Flattop gasped. "It's you, isn't it?"

The horse tossed its mane and whinnied.

" 'Right under my nose until a couple days ago,' huh? Pretty tricky."

The horse pranced around the stall, proudly holding its head up.

"Okay, Wizard. You're hot stuff. Now, could you come out of there? I want to go home."

The horse snorted.

Flattop brushed off the slimy flecks of hay. "Don't be a poor sport! I caught you fair and square!"

The horse shook its head and stamped its hooves.

"Nothing's easy with you, is it?" Flattop sighed, then kicked a pile of straw into a darkened corner and sat down. "Fine. I'll just wait here 'til you give up."

The horse turned its backside to Flattop.

"Sore loser," Flattop mumbled. He leaned against the straw, pulled his cap lower on his brow, and crossed his arms to wait.

20

The velvet touch of the horse's nose pushed on Flattop's face and woke him. He sat up in the straw pile and rubbed his eyes. Hearing men's voices, he peeked out through the stall railing to see Lord Faversham and James.

" 'Twill all be over soon," James said, "and we shall be rid of her."

"How quickly can we arrange the hearing?" asked Lord Faversham.

"Two days. Promptly afterward, Lady Wickshire will be driven from my castle and my lands."

Flattop's mouth dropped open. James was getting rid of Alice, and Rosalinde's father was helping. He pulled himself up to the next railing for a better look.

"What will you require of me?" Faversham asked.

"I shall do most of the talking. I will give them my testimony that she and her family lied to me, and she is really of low birth." James laughed. "No one can expect Lord Wickshire to stay married to a base commoner." He stepped in closer to Faversham. "I shall state my proof—her kindnesses to the serfs, her generosity with my property—she doles out spices and cloth as though they were of no cost. Only a woman of low birth would extend such charity."

"What will you have me say?"

"Testify that you know of her family. That they were not born into nobility but acquired their wealth as merchants."

"Is that true?"

"Of course not. But with your statement and my proof, no one will believe her. Once the marriage is dissolved and Alice is forced to leave my lands, I shall be free to marry Rosalinde."

Faversham nodded. "Very well. I look forward to the day our lands are joined as one, my friend." The two men clasped hands in agreement.

" 'Tis done, then. I will send a messenger to gather the council. Come, let us go to the Great Hall and share some ale in celebration." James led Faversham out the door.

Flattop leaned against the wall. "What am I going to do?" He looked up into the horse's Wizard-eyes. "I don't suppose you'll help me with this." The horse shook its head. "Yeah, right," he said, getting up and brushing the straw off his baseball uniform. "Thanks for nothing," he grumbled as he left the barn.

The sun had almost set, and Flattop shivered. He shoved his hands into his jacket pockets and walked across the inner drawbridge. He didn't want to see James and Lord Faversham celebrating in the Great Hall, so he wandered around the courtyard.

He stood in the doorway of the little chapel. William had stayed in a chapel like this one for his all-night vigil before becoming a knight. He'd prayed for guidance and wisdom and kindness. James must've performed a vigil before he was dubbed, too. A lot of good that did.

Flattop strolled into the garden filled with big, flashy, scarlet red roses. The color of the blood that had dried under William's nose today. Flattop brushed his hand over the soft, red petals. How did Alice stay so nice around people like James and his friends? She wasn't like them at all.

Looking around, he saw a single white rose, growing in a forgotten corner of the garden. *Alice,* he thought. In a world of bright red roses, one lonely white one stood by itself. It wasn't loud or pushy, just simple and pretty and better than the rest because it was one-of-a-kind. "Alice," he whispered.

In a heartbeat, he broke the rose off the stem and ran all the way to the woman outside Alice's chamber door.

He thrust the flower in the woman's face. "Here. I got this for Alice."

She backed up in surprise, then smiled and took the white rose. " 'Tis beautiful. Would you like to see her?"

"Can I?"

"Aye, lad. She has asked for you." The woman opened the bedroom door and motioned for Flattop to step inside.

Alice looked small and weak lying under the indigo covers in her four-poster bed. A strip of red fabric was tied to each of the bedposts. She smiled at him.

Flattop swallowed hard and tiptoed forward. "Hi, Alice." He held out the white rose. "I got this for you."

She took the flower. The twinkle in her green eyes returned as she asked, "Do you want to ask me if I have had the baby yet?"

Flattop laughed. "Nah. I know you did."

"A girl."

"Yeah. I heard."

"Would you like to see her?"

"Sure!"

Alice called for a servant to bring in the baby while Flattop rubbed his sweaty hands on his pants.

The baby was wrapped in cream-colored cloth. Flattop pulled back the stiff fabric and peeked at her. Her face looked kind of bashed in—the way his little cousin Eric had looked right after he was born.

"She is so very beautiful," Alice said.

"Yeah," Flattop lied, as he looked at the baby's flattened nose. "Actually, right now she looks kind of like William."

The servant wrapped the baby and took her back in the other room. Alice looked up at the red cloth strips and was quiet for a long time. "Lord Wickshire is not pleased."

"Does he even know?" Flattop couldn't help sneering.

"Word was sent to the tournament grounds. I have heard no reply."

Flattop guessed James had been too busy humiliating William and plotting against Alice. . . . The plot! Maybe Flattop could warn her. "Alice?" he tested. "Do you . . . *really* like it here?"

" 'Tis my home, Flattop."

"Yeah, I know, but . . . James is kind of a . . . you know. And I think maybe you should move to an apartment somewhere." At least, that's what adults did in his century when they split up.

"An . . . apartment?" Alice propped herself up on her elbows, then grimaced in pain.

Flattop had hoped he could get Alice to leave, but all he'd done was confuse her. "Forget it," he said. "It was a stupid idea. I just thought maybe since James wasn't happy, and if you weren't—"

"James is my husband. I owe him my obedience and my lifelong devotion."

Flattop quickly nodded in agreement. He didn't want to upset her, and now he was embarrassed he'd ever started this conversation. He forced a casual smile. "Yeah. You're right. Like I said, forget it."

Alice studied his face carefully, which made him even more uncomfortable. "Well, I'd better be going. It's getting late and everything." He backed toward the door. "Nice baby." With that, he opened the door and ducked out.

He dragged his cleats through the rushes in the hallway. "It's hopeless," he muttered. "Just give up."

Do something.

Flattop looked around. "Is that you, Wizard?"

Do something.

"What can I do?" he grumbled. "I'm just a kid."

You're a kid with the truth.

Flattop paced up and down the same three steps over and over. "What do you want me to do?" he snapped.

Do something.

Flattop yanked his hat off and scratched his head. He needed help—somebody on his side. Alice was too weak. "William!" He ran to their bedchamber. Certainly William would do it, especially after today.

He barged into the room. "William! Help me!"

William lifted his head from the pillow and slowly looked toward the door. "Flattop? Where have you been?"

"We've got a big problem with your brother."

"Did you fetch me my great helm?"

"Yeah." Flattop looked down and realized he was empty-handed. "I mean, no. But I know where it is."

"I must have it. I trusted you to fetch it for me."

"I know," Flattop said. "But something came up. James is going to have Alice kicked out of the castle. He and Lord Faversham are making up a bunch of lies about her. We've got to stop them!"

"What do you propose *we* do?"

Flattop thought for a moment. "I don't know. You're a knight, think of something!"

William shook his head. "I cannot stand against my brother, Flattop. I have sworn my loyalty to him."

"He beat you up and stole your girlfriend! How loyal is *that*?"

"Lord Wickshire owes me nothing but a roof over my head and food in my belly."

Flattop felt his fists clench. He was ready to punch William right in his broken nose. "You promised to take care of people, to be brave and have honor and stuff like that."

"Aye."

"Well, your own sister-in-law is going to be kicked out and you don't want to help."

William sighed and weakly raised his hand to his forehead. "She is Lord Wickshire's concern. I cannot—"

"And when she's gone, James is going to marry Rosalinde."

With a long, painful groan, William sat up. "What?"

That got him, Flattop congratulated himself. "Now will you help me?"

William gripped one of the thick, round bedposts and pulled himself to a standing position.

Flattop's heart leaped for joy. "You're gonna do it, aren't you? You're gonna help me fight the bad guys!"

William slowly raised his arms to put his hands on

Flattop's shoulders. "Flattop," he said softly, "there are no bad guys."

Flattop felt his ears get hot. He knocked William's hands away. "Fine! I'll do it myself!" he shouted as he stormed to the door.

"Flattop! Wait!" William called out in a strained voice.

"No!" He turned around to glare at William. "Your brother is a bully and you, *Sir* William, are nothing but a big chicken!" He stomped out the door.

William followed. "Wait, my friend—"

"Don't call me that! I am *not* your friend!" Flattop charged down the hallway, hot tears filling his eyes. "Stupid knights!" he muttered. "Stupid Middle Ages!" He slapped the stone walls. "Stupid, dumb castles!"

He rounded the corner by Alice's bedchamber and ran right into James.

"Mind your step, boy," James ordered.

"Don't tell me what to do!" Flattop shouted. "I'm not one of your scaredy-cat little knights! You don't own *me,* buster."

"Flattop!" William called out.

"Shut up, William! You may be afraid of your brother but I'm not." Flattop glared at James. "You're a big man when you can pick on women, aren't you? Tell a bunch of lies and get them kicked out of your castle. Oh yeah, I'm real afraid of you."

"Flattop, don't!" William pleaded in a hoarse whisper.

James looked at William. "Take care of this little pest."

"Aye." William ran down the corridor toward the Great Hall.

"Little pest! Well, that's better than being a big, stupid jerk!'' Flattop shoved James's chest. ''Come on, Mr. Big Shot. Why don't you fight me?''

With one firm push, James knocked Flattop against the wall. ''You had better take your leave, little man,'' James warned through clenched teeth.

Flattop took a threatening stance. ''Come on, you jerk. I've got a little surprise for you. I bet karate hasn't even been invented yet!'' Flattop hadn't actually taken any karate classes, but he had seen a couple of movies. He shifted his weight from one foot to the other and waved his hands menacingly.

''Seize him!'' James shouted over Flattop's head.

Flattop turned to see two knights running through the hallway. Before he could move, they grabbed his arms and dragged him away.

Flattop sat in the mucky, moldy dungeon at Wickshire Castle with rusty, iron cuffs tightly clamped to his wrists and ankles. His outstretched arms were fastened to the wall and his legs were chained to the floor. The walls of the small prison oozed moisture that reflected the firelight from the single torch in a holder by the door.

Flattop rested his head against the cold, slimy wall. Maybe he shouldn't have lost his temper. Maybe he shouldn't have called James a jerk—twice. His dad would've said he'd used "poor judgement."

Flattop closed his eyes. The image that had haunted him for the last few hours returned. He'd been dragged through the storeroom and down the same narrow steps where he'd first heard James reciting poetry to Rosalinde. As the stairs spiraled downward into increasing blackness, he'd looked up at his last glimpse of freedom to see William standing at the top of the stairs. Quietly, calmly watching.

"Are we comfy, then?" Flattop heard the voice at the same time he smelled the blast of sour breath. He opened his eyes to see the guard staring at him and gleefully smiling, showing off the two teeth in his head that weren't broken off or rotted.

"Yes, sir." Flattop forced a smile and tried to be polite. He couldn't afford to offend anyone else.

The man leaned in closer to Flattop, his face a mass of huge red lumps and open sores. "Angered Lord Wickshire, did you?" he asked.

"Yes, sir."

The guard chuckled and scratched his head. When he pulled his hand away, several strands of his thinning white hair came with it. He frowned and shook the hair off his pale, puffy fingers. Flattop watched it float down onto his red satin jacket. The man sighed. "Well. There you have it." He ran his fingers over the shiny surface of Flattop's jacket, then got up and shuffled back to his chair by the door.

Flattop closed his eyes again and the image came back—William standing at the top of the stairs, watching. He opened his eyes and shook his head to erase the mental picture.

He had only himself to blame. He'd told William to shut up. Called him a chicken. Said William wasn't his friend. And now, it looked like that part was true.

After all, William had run to get the other knights. The knights who tossed him into this creepy place with the smelly, weird guard.

Flattop scanned the small room, spotting empty iron cuffs and chains. He was the only prisoner. He'd felt alone before, but this was much, much worse.

A tiny flash of movement in the far right corner caught his eye. He squinted into the shadows and saw a rat crawling over a mound of chains. Flattop shivered.

He liked rats well enough when they were somebody's pet or when a teacher kept them in a classroom. But this was a . . . a real rat. The kind that bites. The kind that eats people's fingers and eyes when they're imprisoned in a dungeon.

Flattop's heart pounded as he watched the rat travel along the stone walls until it bumped into him. It sniffed along his leg, then crawled up onto his ankle. Flattop shook his leg and tried to scare it, but it just grabbed on until he stopped. Then it ran straight for his face.

Flattop closed his eyes, turned his head, and was ready to scream, "Don't eat my eyes!" But the rat stopped when it got to his chest. Flattop opened one eye to see the rat wiggle its whiskers and stare at him. Flattop recognized a familiar glint in its little pink eyes. "Wizard?"

The rat stood up on its hind legs.

"Boy, am I glad to see you."

The rat looked toward the door. Flattop followed its gaze to find the guard had fallen asleep and was softly snoring.

"Get me out of here!" Flattop whispered.

Running to the guard's chair, the rat crawled up on the man's lap and nosed through the keys hanging on his belt. It tried pulling, pushing, and grabbing the keys with its teeth, but they wouldn't budge.

The rat scampered back to Flattop, jumped on his chest, and squeaked.

"What do you mean, you can't get them? You're a Wizard!"

The rat turned a circle on Flattop's stomach, then climbed down, ran behind Flattop, and tugged on his back pocket.

Flattop inched away from the wall to give the Wizard a little more room. His eyes opened wide as he felt tiny paws digging around in his back pocket. Flattop glanced at the sleeping guard, then stifled a laugh. "What the heck are you doing?"

The clicking of the rat's claws on the dark glass was Flattop's answer. "Ohhh. We're going home!" Flattop smiled. The Wizard wasn't such an uncooperative guy, after all. Flattop rolled his hip slightly forward so the rat would have an easier time pulling the dark glass out of his pocket. "Thanks, Wizard. I know I didn't exactly catch you this time, but it's nice of you to bend the rules."

Flattop felt the dark glass slide out of his pocket and hit the floor. "Careful!" he warned. "Now bring it up to my hand."

Instead, the rat used its nose to push the glass over to the guard.

"Pssst! Come back here! Give that to me!"

The rat ran up the guard's leg, across his chest to his face.

"Don't! You traitor!" Flattop hissed.

Looking back, it stood on its hind legs and pushed the guard's cheek with its paws. When the man woke up, it ran down his leg and back and forth across his feet.

"Give it to me, Wizard!" Flattop demanded a little louder.

The guard sat up straight and looked around, wide-eyed. "Wizard?" he asked. "Did—did you say, w—wizard?"

"No," Flattop said, knowing he needed to do more explaining than that. But all he could think of was that his ticket home was about to be discovered. He tried not to look at the dark glass on the floor. Instead, he looked at the guard and smiled as bright a smile as he could muster. "I said . . . wiz . . . something. I don't remember what I said."

Boy, was that bad, his mind judged.

The rat squeaked.

The guard looked down at his feet. "Well, if it isn't my little friend," he said.

His "little friend" scurried to the dark glass and cirled it, squeaking over and over.

The man reached down and picked up the dark glass. "What have we here?"

Flattop went numb. He couldn't feel anything except a dull, hollow pain where his heart used to be. William had deserted him, and now the Wizard had betrayed him.

"Thank you, little friend," the guard said. He turned the glass over in his hand. "What is this?" he asked Flattop as he held it up to the torch light.

The words shattered in the distant reaches of Flattop's mind and lost their meaning. Flattop shook his head and looked away. A huge, spiked ball of emotion scratched its way up his throat. It stung his eyes and quivered his lip.

"Well, now! Aren't you a handsome man!" The Wizard's voice said. The guard stared open-mouthed into the dark glass.

"A wizard!" the man finally said.

"Yeah," Flattop answered.

"Is he very powerful?"

A tiny ray of hope shone through Flattop's despair. *Don't give up! Keep thinking! Talk!* Flattop just said the first words that came to mind. "He's a very powerful wizard. More powerful than—than ten Lord Wickshires."

The man wiped a dirty, ragged sleeve across his mouth, and looked into the glass again.

Flattop realized his only chance at freedom rested with the dark glass. "But he'll only follow *my* orders. Unless . . ."

"Unless what?" The guard looked at Flattop.

"Unless I give the glass to you."

The old man gasped. "To me?"

Flattop nodded. "But you'll have to let me go." Fear gnawed at his insides. He was giving up his ticket home. But if he didn't get out of this dungeon, he'd never get home anyway.

The guard scowled into the glass.

"Just think, good fellow," the Wizard said. "I could be all yours."

"I do not know about any of this." He scratched at the red lumps on his face.

The Wizard spoke again. "You have it on the best authority that a sizeable sum of gold is headed your way right this moment."

The man gasped again. "Gold?"

"Aye, but you must release the boy."

With a jingle of keys, the guard stood up, put the dark glass on the chair, and shuffled over to Flattop. In a matter of seconds, the cuffs and chains were unlocked, and Flattop was holding his arms at his sides for the first time in hours.

The man quickly unlocked the door, then picked up the dark glass and pointed it at Flattop. "There, Wizard. See? The boy is free."

Flattop straightened his baseball cap and said, "Thank you, sir." He ran out the door and up the slippery, wet steps. Halfway up the spiral stairway, he bumped into Alice and knocked her off balance. With shaky hands she clutched at the stone wall.

"Alice! Are you all right?" Flattop grabbed her arm to steady her. "What're you doing out of bed?"

"I heard a certain gallant young noble had fought bravely for my honor and was in need of assistance," she said, smiling weakly.

Flattop beamed. "You mean me? I'm fine now. I escaped."

"I see that." She touched his shoulder. "Go to the livery. There is a wagon waiting there."

"But, Alice—"

"Do as I say! I shall join you in a moment." She lifted a small purple bag tied with a black string. "I brought some gold to buy your guard's cooperation. He will need it to move his family from Wickshire."

Flattop gasped. "The gold!"

Alice urged him forward. "Off with you! We do not have much time before my husband awakes and finds us gone."

"*Us?* You're coming, too?"

"Aye. Now, to the livery with you."

Flattop scrambled up the steps, ran across the inner drawbridge, and burst into the livery, panting for breath.

There, inside the big, hinged barn doors, he saw a wagon hitched to two horses. It was filled with a wooden chest, a cradle, and two saddles. Beside it stood William, whispering and cooing into a bundle of cream-colored fabric.

"William! What're you doing here?"

"I am helping my sister-in-law and her baby to safety." He raised his eyebrows and flashed a crooked smile. "Not to mention a hot-headed friend who has of late displeased my brother."

Feeling his cheeks burn with embarrassment, Flattop looked at the ground. "I acted like a jerk, huh?"

William chuckled. "If a *jerk* is a stubborn fool who does not know when to hold his tongue, then you are a jerk."

"I'm sorry."

"Do not apologize for trying to do what was good

and honorable." The baby started to whimper. William bounced her gently. "You would make a fine knight, Flattop Kincaid."

"Thanks. You're not so bad yourself." Flattop glanced out the open doors. "What's James going to say when he finds out you helped us?"

William shrugged. "I plan to leave with you."

"You do? Where are we going?"

"I shall accompany you as far as the convent. There, Alice will be able to raise Wickshire's only heir in safety. After that, we will unhitch the horses, and you and I will ride to the Hart's Blood Inn. Alice assures me that Blanche will care for you."

"Where'll *you* go?" Flattop asked.

"I am not sure. But now that I have stood against Lord Wickshire, I must become a knight errant." William smiled. "I shall wander the land competing in tournaments and searching for a lord who is worthy of my loyalty."

Alice entered the barn, stopping to grab the doorway and lean into the wood until she caught her breath. William and Flattop helped her into the back of the wagon and laid the baby in the cradle. Then they jumped onto the bench seat in front.

William picked up the reins and slapped them. "To the future," he declared.

"Aye, to the future," Alice said softly.

Flattop forced a smile, trying to look positive. But without his dark glass, the future was the last thing he wanted to think about.

The wagon slowly pulled out of the barn and across the outer drawbridge, while Alice steadied the cradle so her baby would sleep.

22

The black of night surrendered to the blue-gray of early morning as the wagon pitched and rattled across the countryside. Alice had fallen asleep, bundled in a fur-lined cloak.

The baby, who had been peacefully sleeping, started to whimper. Flattop sat up on his knees and peered into the cradle. "Hey," he whispered. "Don't cry, okay?"

"My baby," Alice mumbled, her eyes half-open.

"She's okay. She's probably just a little cranky."

Alice struggled to sit up and reach into the cradle.

"Here, let me get her," Flattop said. He studied the baby for a long moment, trying to remember how to pick her up without her head falling off or something. He pushed the sleeves of his jacket up, took a deep breath, and reached into the cradle. With one hand under the baby's neck and head and the other on her lower back, he slowly, carefully lifted her like she was a bomb about to explode.

He placed her in Alice's arms, then breathed a sigh of relief and wiped the newly formed sweat off his brow.

"Flattop? Why is your wrist banded?" Alice asked.

"Banded?" He looked down at his arms and saw the

black plastic of his waterproof sports watch. He'd been careful to keep it hidden so people wouldn't torture him for practicing witchcraft. But he decided to risk telling Alice the truth.

He glanced up at William in the driver's seat of the wagon and was happy to see that his friend wasn't the least bit interested in Flattop's "banded wrist." Flattop stepped across the cradle to sit close to Alice. He unfastened the watch and showed it to her. "It's called a watch."

Reaching out to touch it, she asked, "What does it do?"

"It tells the time. Like midnight or two o'clock."

Alice looked at him like he was crazy.

"It's a stopwatch, too," he added, then demonstrated how it worked. Flattop thought he saw fear in her eyes as she watched the digital numbers in the tenths-of-seconds spot flashing by. "Don't be scared," he said, fastening the watch to his wrist again. "Everyone in California has one of these." Even though she nodded, she still looked a little afraid.

William pulled up to the convent next to Quentin's monastery and began to unload the wagon. "I'll unhitch the cart and saddle our horses if you will see to Alice."

"Sure," Flattop said, performing a two-handed vault over the side of the wagon. With the help of some of the nuns, he eased Alice out of the wagon and helped her walk to the big, beige-colored building. Others followed behind, carrying the wooden chest and cradle.

They walked through the door, down a long corridor and into a tiny bedroom. Flattop walked Alice to the only chair in the room. She sat down, leaned against the straight-backed, dark wood, and brushed her hand across her forehead.

One of the nuns cradled the baby in her arms. "By what name shall you christen this child?"

"She is but one day old," Alice said. "I know not what name to give her."

"How about Alison?" Flattop volunteered.

Alice and all the nuns looked at him.

He swallowed hard. "It's a pretty cool name in California."

"You must miss your California," Alice said with a sigh.

"Yeah." A painful stab of homesickness pierced his heart. His California was a wonderful place. And unless he could get the dark glass back, he would never see it again.

Flattop looked up to see William in the doorway. "Come, Flattop," he said softly. "We must leave."

Turning toward Alice, Flattop looked into her green eyes. "Well," he said, shrugging. "I gotta go." He looked around the tiny, stone-walled room. "You sure you'll be okay here?"

She took his hand and, holding it tightly, stood up. "I shall be fine. I have been sending money here for several years, in case I needed a place to stay."

"You have?"

"Aye," she said. "You do not think Lord Wickshire's interest in Rosalinde was the first of its kind, do you?"

Flattop shrugged. "He wants to marry her to get all her land."

" 'Tis true." Alice nodded. "But her father is not the wealthy noble he appears. Why would he want to marry his daughter to someone with less land than he owns? 'Tis not sound business."

"How do you know all that?"

"When you are kind to people, they repay you with kindness—sometimes in the form of information."

William walked over to Alice. "You can be sure," he said, "in my role as knight errant, that I shall keep informed of Lord Wickshire's actions. When the time is right, I shall strike a blow for justice and return Wickshire to its rightful heir, your daughter."

"I happily await that day, Sir William," Alice said, beaming with pride.

Turning to face the nuns, William bowed slightly. "We must take our leave now, good sisters." He walked out of the room, glancing over his shoulder. "Come, Flattop."

Come, Flattop. Here we go again, Flattop thought. He kissed Alice's hand and they both laughed. But he couldn't make himself say good-bye. "See ya' around."

Alice nodded. "Aye, lad." Even though she was smiling, Flattop thought he saw tears in her eyes. A strange emotion choked Flattop's throat as he followed William out of the convent to the place where their horses were saddled and ready to go. Alice wasn't that far away from the Hart's Blood Inn, he told himself. He could ride over to see her once in awhile. Without the Wizard's dark glass, he certainly wasn't going home soon.

Trying to cheer himself up, he focused on positive thoughts. Staying at Blanche's for awhile wouldn't be so bad. After all, she was a nice lady. And she made great sausages.

He hoisted himself onto his horse and followed William to the gate.

"Flattop!" Alice called out.

He pulled back on the reins and saw her struggling to run toward him.

"I almost forgot," she said, reaching into a pouch tied on her belt. "The castle guard asked me to return this to you." She pulled out the dark glass and handed it up to him.

Flattop had to remind himself to breathe. He did his best not to let his fingers shake as he reached for the purple-y black glass that would carry him home.

Alice came closer and spoke softly so no one else would hear. "The guard said it was enchanted—that it held a wizard. But after you left, it held only frightful images of fire-breathing monsters and demons."

"Really?" Flattop looked into the glass, but saw nothing. He stuffed it into his back pocket, swearing to never surrender it again. "Well . . . it's kind of important to me, so thanks for giving it back."

"Flattop, come," William said, with a hint of impatience in his voice.

Flattop smiled at Alice. "I gotta go before he has a cow."

Alice furrowed her brow. Flattop shrugged his shoulders. "That's what we say in California."

Alice smiled, her green eyes twinkling. "Well then, go safely before you both have cows."

Flattop laughed and followed William out through the convent gate. He turned around one last time and waved good-bye to Alice, knowing it probably would be for good.

After a couple of handball games with Quentin at the monastery, William and Flattop rode to the town. As they trotted through the wooden gates, Flattop wrinkled his nose. The place was as smelly as ever. They stabled their horses and walked to the Hart's Blood Inn.

The sweet aroma of Blanche's sausages was a welcome change for their noses. At supper, Flattop smashed his sausages into his boiled potatoes while William and Blanche discussed business. William acted as Alice's representative and worked out a deal for Flattop to stay with Blanche.

From now on, they agreed, Flattop would act as an apprentice. He would get up at sunrise, help make the food and brew the ale, then clear the tables and wait on customers. At night, after he cleaned the inn, he would be allowed to sleep on one of the tables.

By the time Blanche and William had finished their business dealings, Flattop had polished off a second helping of sausages. All the men and women gathered around to hear William's gallant stories about the tournament. Flattop sat next to him, nodding his agreement at every exciting point in the story. Of course, William didn't mention that his brother had beaten him up so badly he practically needed a can opener to get out of his helmet.

William told them about all the swords and shields he'd ransomed, then opened a pouch full of gold and jewels. "Good woman!" he shouted to Blanche. "Bring us tankards of your finest ale!" That made William the most popular guy in the place.

Hours later, the customers left and William staggered up the stairs to his room, leaving Flattop to wipe the tables and sweep the floor. Blanche dumped the garbage into the street and told Flattop that she'd teach him how to make sausages in the morning.

His chores completed, Flattop jumped up on one of the tables and pulled an old horse blanket over his shoulders. He told himself that once he caught the Wizard and went home, he'd make homemade sausages for breakfast. He closed his eyes and fell asleep listening to the town watchman calling, "Cover fire!"

Flattop woke to dim sunlight and an awful odor that made his eyes water. He sat up slowly, rubbing his sore shoulders and stiff neck. Too many nights in a bed had made him soft.

"Up with you, lad!" Blanche called from behind him. "There is much to be done." He turned and saw her standing at the fireplace, stirring a big, black cauldron. "Come here and tend this pot," she said, holding out the long, wooden stick she used as a cook spoon.

Rubbing his eyes, he walked to the hearth and took over. He peered into the kettle. It didn't contain sausages, but whatever boiled inside was the stinkiest stuff he'd ever smelled. It made his empty stomach turn. Even the sewage and rotting garbage outside smelled better than this.

He pulled the stick out of the steaming brew. With it came a blob of dark blue fabric. "Hey! This is indigo, huh?"

"Aye, lad."

"How come it stinks so much?"

" 'Tis not the indigo you smell." Blanche carried over a hammered metal chamber pot and poured the dark yellow contents into the cauldron. " 'Tis the urine."

Flattop jumped back in horror. "The what?"

"The morning urine of young boys. 'Tis the secret to setting the dye at its darkest color."

"You mean you just dump it in?"

"Oh no, lad!" Blanche laughed. "It has to be aged six weeks before it can be used."

Flattop cringed as he thought about the indigo covers on the bed at Wickshire. William had told him there was a "very special process" to get the color that dark. All Flattop wanted to do now was wash his hands. He walked to the doorway and glanced down the street, hoping he'd get lucky and the Wizard would be right outside.

Nope. No Wizard.

Blanche let him off the hook and told him he could make the sausages instead. Flattop eagerly agreed to do anything that didn't involve indigo.

She stationed him at a chopping table next to a metal grinder and a big bowl. She tossed a slab of red meat from a cloth-covered container onto the table. Even in the dim, early morning light, Flattop could see a pale green rainbow on one side of it. At his house, meat like that got thrown away.

She slapped a loaf of bread onto the table. It skidded across the wood planks and fell to the floor, scattering crumbs as it hit. Blanche sighed, picked up the loaf, and put it back on the table. Then she scooped up the crumbs from the floor and threw them into the bowl. Flattop had to tell himself to close his mouth and not act shocked.

Chunks of ham that were dried-out and discolored around the edges were tossed into the bowl, along with two gloppy handfuls of last night's water-logged potatoes. Then a portion of cheese with blue-green mold on one side was added. With every new item, Flattop was more convinced he'd never eat sausage again.

A ray of hope burned brightly as Blanche lifted the lid on a small kettle and scooped some porridge into the sausage mixture. Flattop was almost certain the porridge was safe. After Blanche ground up the whole mess, she added spices from her locked cabinet. Then she stuffed the mixture into a slimy, thin casing—which Flattop discovered was animal intestines.

When William stumbled downstairs for his farewell meal of Blanche's homemade sausage, Flattop had to stop himself from shuddering every time William took a bite.

Later, he walked William to the livery and waited as his friend saddled up to leave him for good. "William?"

"What?"

Flattop pulled off his cap, hit it against his thigh, and watched the dust fly. "I just want you to know that . . . you did the right thing by helping Alice."

A half-smile crossed William's face. "Well, we shall see." He turned his horse to leave the stable.

"William! Wait!" Flattop had a sudden urge to confess everything—his time travel, his parents, his baseball team. "If you ever come back and I'm not here, don't worry about me, okay?"

"What?"

"Because I'm not from here and I may have to go home. See, I live in the future and we have stuff like computers—"

"And watches . . . and enchanted dark glasses."

Flattop gasped. "You *were* listening in the wagon!"

Looking away for a moment, William sighed. "It would be best if you did not share your information about California with others." He nudged his heels into the side of his horse and trotted toward the gate. "Quentin and Alice both know you are here," he said over his shoulder. "If they need you, I have instructed them to send a messenger."

Jogging alongside, Flattop asked, "What about James?"

"I do not think my brother will seek you out. He is just as happy to have you gone. However, should you need sanctuary, go to the monastery. The brothers will protect you."

"Okay," Flattop said, clasping William's hand.

"It has been my pleasure to ride with you, Flattop Kincaid. God be with you."

"You, too," Flattop said.

William spurred his horse and galloped away.

You, too? Flattop's mind scolded. *That's it?* "Thanks for being my friend," he added as he watched William disappear over the ridge.

23

That night, Flattop lay on one of the tables in the Hart's Blood Inn. It had been a long day and he was bone tired. He realized that he'd spent his very first medieval days eating porridge and sleeping on a table in a serf's hut. Now, he was eating porridge and sleeping on a table at an inn.

"Cover fire!" the town watchman cried out.

Flattop closed his eyes and sighed. It was definitely time to go home. Tomorrow he'd check the eyes of every animal in town until he found the Wizard.

"Cover fire, my boy!" the watchman shouted just as Flattop started to drift off to sleep.

My boy?

Flattop's eyes flew open and he sat up with a jolt. "The Wizard!" he whispered. He jumped off the table, charged out the door and ran right into him.

The Wizard stumbled to the ground and moaned. "In the future, my boy, just say, 'I've found you.' "

"Sorry." Flattop helped him struggle to his feet and brushed off the old man's long pants and dark tunic. "Hey! Where's your robe?"

"Well, I can't be much of a town watchman in purple velvet now, can I?"

"I guess not." Flattop reached into his pocket, pulled out the dark glass, and held it up. "Come on, let's go."

"Well, well," the Wizard said in a huff. "No 'Hello, how are you?' No 'Gosh, I hope I didn't break any of your bones!' "

Flattop sighed. "Wizard!"

"Oh, all right," the Wizard grumbled, raising his hand. "Let's get this over with."

"Flattop!" a vaguely familiar voice called to him through the darkness. "Flattop Kincaid!" Quentin galloped toward him on horseback.

An uncertain fear clenched Flattop's stomach. "What's wrong?"

" 'Tis Alice. She's taken sick with the fever. She has asked for you."

Alarm bells sounded in every part of Flattop's body. Fever killed people. Torn between two worlds, Flattop looked at the dark glass, then back at the Wizard. "I— I can't go . . . now."

The Wizard shrugged. "Catch me later?"

Flattop considered the possibilities. What if he couldn't catch the Wizard? What if he lost the dark glass again?

What if Alice died?

Flattop turned to Quentin. "Let's go!"

With help from a stable boy, Flattop's horse was saddled in no time, and he followed Quentin through the town gate. His horse galloped so fast, Flattop thought it would topple over in a forward somersault.

As they crested the hill above the monastery and convent, the fear climbed from Flattop's stomach to clutch at his heart. Was it possible that by helping Flattop escape, Alice had put her own life in danger? He had seen a movie once about a time traveler who had affected the future by things he did in the past. It occurred to him that if Alice died, her baby might die, too.

Alison Wedertz might never be born. He wiped off the cold sweat that suddenly formed above his lip. Sometimes Alison Wedertz could be a bossy know-it-all, but she wasn't the worst girl in his school. By far.

And now, thanks to him, she might not even exist.

Quentin and Flattop entered the convent gate and jumped down from their horses. Flattop ran into the convent and followed a nun to Alice's room.

She lay in bed, still as death, under a pile of covers. One of the nuns sat beside her, dabbing at her forehead with a wet cloth. Flattop tiptoed over to the bed. Even in the warm glow of the candlelight, Alice looked pale, and had dark circles under her closed eyes.

"Alice?" Flattop said softly.

She opened her eyes and offered a weak smile. "Flattop, I have a fever."

"Yeah. I heard." He tried to sound as cheerful as he could.

She motioned for him to lean in closer. "The sisters . . . they have no red," she whispered.

"*No red* what?"

"Cloth . . . red cloth." She tilted her head and looked at one of the bedposts. "Red."

"Oh!" Flattop said. "Red cloth for the bedposts?"

She barely nodded.

Flattop looked down at his uniform, then peeled off his jacket. "Wait!" he said. "I've got the perfect thing!" He grabbed hold of the red cotton shoulder of his long-sleeved T-shirt and yanked as hard as he could. It took a couple of good tugs, but he managed to tear it off. Then he attacked the other sleeve.

Tearing the red fabric into four strips, he tied them

to Alice's bedposts. She smiled and whispered, "Thank you." Then she closed her eyes.

A nun entered the room carrying a metal bowl and a knife.

"What are you going to do with that?" Flattop asked.

"Bleed her," the woman answered. " 'Twill take some of the poison out."

Flattop stepped in front of Alice's bed. "No. That doesn't help. You'll just make her sicker."

"Flattop," Alice said. "Let her."

"But, Alice—"

"Please," she whispered.

Flattop finally stepped aside and the nun moved to the bed. She carefully turned Alice's palm up and pushed the sleeve of her tunic aside. The nun chose a vein that showed up bright blue on Alice's arm, then slowly drove the tip of the blade into the skin.

Alice closed her eyes tightly and gritted her teeth. Flattop felt his hands clench into fists. In the next instant, a steady trickle of dark red blood started to flow out of Alice's arm and into the bowl.

Flattop had seen lots of scary movies where people ended up all bloody, but seeing the real thing made his head spin. He had to back up and lean against the wall so he wouldn't fall down. After a few minutes, the nun tied a cloth around Alice's arm and left the room with a bowl full of blood.

Alice tried to pull the covers up higher. "Flattop," she said, her teeth beginning to chatter. "Tell me about your California."

Flattop picked up his jacket off the floor and handed it to Alice. "Okay. But wear this for now. It's pretty warm. Plus it's red."

She dragged it under the pile of blankets. "Thank you," she said, then drifted off to sleep.

Everyone else left the room. Flattop sat in a chair by Alice's bed and told her all about California—and his century. Cars, computers, refrigerators, movies, and TV. Even though Alice was unconscious, it felt good to finally tell her the truth. After a couple of hours, she began to toss and turn, and sweat poured down her face. Flattop wiped it off with the wet cloth the nun had used.

He told Alice about school—and Alison Wedertz. And why she had to get well so her baby would live and Alison would be born centuries from now. Eventually he was all talked out, and Alice was resting quietly. He stared at the wall, sighed, and closed his eyes.

"Flattop?" Alice's voice woke him up.

"Yeah?" he said, rubbing his eyes. He looked up to see a couple of nuns propping some pillows behind Alice's back so she could sit up.

"The fever is gone," Alice said, smiling. Though she still looked pale and weak, her green eyes had gotten back some of their sparkle. "They tell me you were with me all night."

Flattop shrugged, a little ashamed that he'd fallen asleep. "Yeah. I tried to stay awake."

"You are indeed a friend, loyal and true."

"I am? I mean . . . thank you." He felt his cheeks get hot with embarrassment.

"No, lad. Thank *you*." She reached out her hand and Flattop kissed it, like he always did.

And she laughed, like she always did.

"Flattop," Alice said, "Please do not think me strange, but I had the most curious dream last night." She whispered, "I traveled to an enchanted land."

"Fevers make you have weird dreams," Flattop told her.

"The people spoke such a peculiar language." She shook her head. "Have you ever heard of a . . . computer?"

Flattop felt all the blood drain out of his head. Somehow his all-night confession had gotten through to her. "A computer," he repeated. "Well . . . It's . . . We have them in California, and—" He grinned sheepishly. "Some people travel in them."

"Oh," was all she said.

The nuns came in with some bread and cheese, announcing that Alice needed her rest. Flattop left the room and strolled down the convent hall. He was glad he'd chosen to stay and help Alice get over her fever. He reached in his back pocket and ran his thumb along the edge of the dark glass. He was quick and strong. He'd get another chance to go home.

Two nuns walked by with their dark hoods completely shading their faces. They folded their arms, tucking their hands inside the sleeves of their tunics. "Good morning," he said, as they passed him. When they didn't answer, he turned to watch them walk away.

Another nun hurried past. With her hood pulled up over her bowed head Flattop could barely see the long, white beard that—

Beard?

Flattop reached out and caught the Wizard's arm. "I've found you," he said, just like the Wizard had asked him to do.

"That's much better, Marvin, my boy," the Wizard said with a chuckle.

Flattop took out the dark glass and touched it to the Wizard's hand. The moment he saw the connection he realized—too late—that Alice still had his red satin jacket. "Wait!" he heard himself shout.

Then everything went black.

Tap, tap, tap.

"Hey, Marvin?"

Tap, tap, tap.

Flattop lifted his head off the computer keyboard just as his dad opened the door and walked into the bedroom.

"Dad. It's you."

"Yeah, I got home early. Your mother said to check on you." He glanced around the room. "What's going on? I've been knocking and knocking."

Flattop couldn't answer. He was too busy trying to make up an explanation for his missing jacket. He finally blurted out, "I don't know what happened to my jacket."

His dad's brow furrowed. "It looks okay to me."

Flattop glanced down. Sure enough, his jacket looked just fine.

"What's wrong with it?" his dad asked.

Flattop bit his lip. "Wrong?" he stalled. "I don't know. It . . . uh . . . felt funny. But now . . . it doesn't." He waved his hand nervously in front of his face. "Never mind. It—it's stupid."

"Okay," his father said, sounding a little suspicious. "Do you have a game today?"

"No. Why?"

"You're in your uniform."

"Oh . . . yeah." Flattop hated these *think fast* situations. "I was just trying it on, in case . . . in case it felt funny. You know, like my jacket did." Flattop was proud that he'd tied both lies together.

His dad raised his eyebrows, then shook his head and shrugged. "Well, Mom says we're eating early tonight because she's got a PTA meeting."

"Okay. Thanks."

His dad paused a second, then shut the door, leaving him alone with the cartoon Wizard on the monitor. Flattop looked at the purple-y black glass in his hand, then back at the Wizard.

Answers to his questions. That's all he wanted. Did something bad happen to James? Did Alice ever return to Wickshire? Did William find fame and fortune as a knight errant? He hoped so. He tucked the dark glass into his back pocket.

"Hey, Wizard. Thanks for bringing back my jacket," he whispered to the screen.

"My pleasure. It was a mere oversight on your part."

Flattop took it off and gently draped it over the back of his chair. That's when he noticed his arms were bare. "My sleeves! Where are my sleeves?"

"Oops!" The Wizard raised his cartoon hand to his mouth. "A mere oversight on *my* part."

"Great," Flattop muttered, then tugged his jacket back on. He didn't feel like explaining missing sleeves to nosy parents.

The Wizard folded his arms and scowled. "I got you home, didn't I?"

"Yeah," Flattop agreed. "But how does everything end? What happens to William and Alice and James and everybody?"

The Wizard shrugged. "Their lives go on, just as yours does."

"But does the story have a happy ending?"

The Wizard smiled. "My boy, this is an adventure.

171

It doesn't have an ending." In a poof of cartoon smoke, the Wizard disappeared from the screen.

"Wait! Come back!" Flattop shouted.

"Marvin!" His dad's voice drifted down the hallway and through his closed door. "Telephone!"

Telephone. Flattop slumped in his chair. He was home. Back in his very own century where his friends could call him to ride bikes, go to the movies, or just hang around and watch TV. Phone calls held exciting possibilities.

Flattop heard his dad's footsteps grow nearer, then the click of his bedroom door opening.

"Alison Wedertz is on the phone," his dad said. "She wants to work on some project tomorrow after school."

That hadn't been one of the exciting possibilities. "Tell her—"

"I'm not your answering service," his dad grumbled as he walked down the hall. "You come out here and tell her yourself."

Flattop sighed and stood up. As he trudged down the hall, images flooded his brain. The green of the Wickshire hillside. The green of Alice's eyes. The green of William's tunic and shield—and the cruel brother who gave them to him. He saw William, Alice, her newborn baby, and their escape from Wickshire.

The *real* story of Alison's ancestors.

As he picked up the receiver, a thought occurred to him. He'd trusted Alice with information from this century. Could he risk telling Alison Wedertz about his medieval adventures?

Flattop thought he heard the Wizard's voice in the back of his brain. *Risk is at the heart of every adventure, my boy.*